A Simmering Dilemma

A SIMMERING DILEMMA

Tyora Moody

A Simmering Dilemma
A Eugeena Patterson Mystery, Book 4

Copyright © 2020 by Tyora Moody

A *Simmering Dilemma* is a work of fiction. Names, characters, places and incidents either are products of the author's imagination or are used fictitiously. Any resemblance to actual persons, living or dead, events, or locales is entirely coincidental.

Paperback ISBN-13: 978-1-7336967-6-0
ePub ISBN-13: 978-1-7336967-7-7

Published by Tymm Publishing LLC
PO Box 8384
1600 Assembly St
Columbia, SC 29202
www.tymmpublishing.com

Cover Design: TywebbinCreations.com
Copy Editing/Proofreading: Felicia Murrell

Dedication

*This book is dedicated to my dear friend and
college roommate, Audrey Riley. She introduced me
to my Lord and Savior, Jesus Christ. I know you are
resting in His arms right now. I will always be
thankful for your precious friendship.*

Acknowledgements

Eugeena is back! This character has been with me over a decade, and I can't believe this is book number four. I started writing *Deep Fried Trouble* in 2008. Five years later, readers were introduced to Eugeena once *Deep Fried Trouble* was published in 2013. While I'm still not quite in her age range, I'm older myself, drawing closer to the day I can retire. Believe me, I don't plan to take up being an amateur sleuth, but I hope to have many, many more books with her and her growing circle of family and friends.

I want to thank my editor, Felicia Murrell for lending her eyes and expertise to this current adventure. I can't thank you enough for your editing skills. No writer ever reaches the stage where they don't need to continue to grow and you definitely help guide that growth process.

I want to thank my mom, who is a number one fan of Eugeena. My mom is an avid reader and her words of wisdom are often built into this character. It brings me great joy to write stories she enjoys. I appreciate her letting me share ideas with her.

Eugeena has developed quite a fanbase from the first three books. A part of that comes from the talents of Sharell Palmer who I've worked with as the narrator for the audiobook versions. When I heard her voice, I felt so connected to her. I thought to myself, "She sounds like the Eugeena in my head." It's been a joy to make sure those who do better with listening to a story have this medium to enjoy. I look forward to working with Sharell in the future on more audiobooks.

Lastly, a huge thanks to all my readers, especially the book clubs. I've met with quite a few of you and I'm always so tickled to hear how much you enjoy Eugeena. I knew back in 2008, there was something special about this character and I'm thankful to God for the opportunity to share her stories. Although there is usually a dead body in most of them, I hope readers see Eugeena's faith and her passion for helping others shine through too.

Cast of Characters

Sugar Creek is a fictional neighborhood in Charleston, South Carolina. In *A Simmering Dilemma*, readers will find many familiar supporting characters from previous Eugeena Patterson mysteries. Just in case you need a reminder of who is who, refer to this list below. I promise that any character introduced from the Sugar Creek neighborhood has something to contribute to the story. I hope you enjoy dropping by the neighborhood for a visit. Ms. Eugeena appreciates you joining the adventure.

Recurring Characters from the Series

(listed according to appearance)
Detective Sarah Wilkes
Annie Mae Brown (Missionary Baptist Church, volunteer)
Willie Mae Brown (Missionary Baptist Church, volunteer)
Amani Gladstone (precocious student in summer program)
Louise Hopkins (Eugeena's next door neighbor)
Jocelyn Miller (Louise's granddaughter)

Eugeena's Family

Ralph Patterson, Jr. (oldest son married to Judy, twin boys, Jacob and Joseph, girl, Jasmine)
Cedric Patterson (son married to Carmen Alpine-Patterson)

Leesa Patterson (daughter, single, two children, Kisha and Tyric)

Amos's Family
Alexa Jones-McCormick (oldest daughter lives in Seattle with son, Douglas)
Briana Jones (youngest daughter has moved into old family home next door)

Eugeena's Aunts
Cora Gibson (aunt closest in age to Eugeena)
Esther Gibson (oldest living aunt)

Chapter 1

One of my favorite proverbs states, "A happy heart makes the face cheerful." I could truly say I've never been happier in all my life. It's been five months since I officially became Eugeena Patterson-Jones. I married my next door neighbor on a Saturday in February, and I know other newlyweds could relate to my joy. But, I'm no ordinary newlywed. I'm sixty-one years old, and I enjoy taking advantage of my AARP and other senior citizens' discounts. Pending social security, my world consists of retirement activities, and oh yeah, sharing my home with a man again. I'd been a widow for five years.

A few years ago, I couldn't have imagined that, at my age, the man I'd secretly had a crush on would become my second husband. The Lord does work in mysterious ways. He could surprise even an old bird like me.

After much discussion, Amos officially moved into the home where I'd raised my three children. His home where he'd resided alone after his wife's death remained empty, and Amos pondered putting the house on the market after he moved in with me.

Until three months ago.

After living in California, trying to make it as a singer,

Amos's youngest daughter moved back home. She'd showed up to surprise her father for Easter Sunday. Next thing we knew, she seemed to remain in Charleston long after her impromptu visit. Amos hadn't turned off the utilities yet, so Briana embraced her parents' former home and appeared to have placed her life in California behind her. This all happened pretty fast and I can't say I was completely comfortable with our new neighbor.

Briana had a rough few years during and after her mom's battle with breast cancer. Perhaps being in the house where her mother last lived provided some comfort. Amos kept many reminders of Francine Jones in the house. After a lengthy estrangement from her father, I recognized that Briana needed him in her life. Just because our children grow up and get their own lives doesn't mean they stop needing us.

Right now, I wasn't sure how well I could remain supportive. For the second night in a row, music blasted from next door into our bedroom. With no cares of this being a Sunday evening, the heavy bass and thumping penetrated right through the window. I thought the windows would shatter at some point.

Next to me, Amos wrestled with the covers on the bed. I knew he was restraining himself from going over to visit his baby girl. In not so many words, before we retired for the night, he'd expressed that he didn't miss the drama that came with facing his youngest daughter.

I knew about drama, having birthed a drama queen myself. The difference was my youngest child and daughter lived across town and showed up occasionally when she needed free babysitting. Leesa was a twenty-three year-old single mom with two young children.

Thank goodness her party days ended the moment she delivered her first child at age seventeen.

Briana was twenty-six with no children and clearly had no intentions of settling down.

"I need to go over there." Amos's voice was gruff, concealing more anger than I knew he had.

I propped myself on my elbow. "Is that really a good idea? Last time didn't go so well."

Last time was the previous night. I wanted to march over to the house myself, but knew I needed to let Amos handle it. Amos tried, but that's not what happened. All I heard was yelling and screaming. Not from Amos. Amos was the silent type who kept his thoughts inside and his face grim. Briana, on the other hand, was livid. And despite the fact she was living in her parents' home rent-free, she insisted Amos had no right to tell her what to do.

There was so much on my mind, but I held my tongue. Besides, this was my fault. Last Christmas, I'd encouraged Amos to reach out to his daughters. After Amos's first wife died, his precarious relationship with both daughters had faded to almost nonexistent. I wanted both of our families to come together before Amos and I officially married. It seemed like the right thing to do.

His oldest daughter, Alexa still lived across the country in Seattle, but kept in touch a lot more. This summer, we were promised time with Douglas, Amos's grandson. All appeared to be healed and improving with his oldest daughter.

Amos's youngest daughter was another whole situation.

The mattress sprang as Amos jumped up from the bed. He turned the lamp on, illuminating the side of the bedroom with the window. "I can't take this anymore,

Eugeena. I'm about to think the girl is doing this on purpose."

I didn't want to agree with him, but I was thinking the same thing.

As soon as Amos had pulled on his pants, the music stopped. We peered at each other. Loud voices drifted up to our window, and then we heard the sounds of car doors slamming and engines revving.

I blinked, "Maybe the party is over." Not that there should have been one at all. Didn't any of the people over there work? It was a Sunday night for crying out loud. Sundays were supposed to be for rest, so people could ease into the work week.

Amos grunted. "I guess there's hope for that girl after all."

I was feeling even more suspicious. Kind of weird how everything stopped when Amos turned on the light. I kept that to myself, though I really wanted to blurt it out loud.

With a swiftness that defied his age, Amos undressed and returned to bed. With the lights out, I edged closer to his warm body as he wrapped his arm around me. I have to say this was one of my favorite parts about being married and something I missed.

I'm not sure how long after we both drifted back to sleep, but noise shrilled from the bedside next to Amos. It was his phone.

He reached over to grab it.

I listened, my eyes slipping back closed, desperately wanting my sleep that had been snatched away. As Amos's conversation started to penetrate my ears, my eyes popped open again.

He'd sat up, raising his voice in a panic. "You found what, Briana?"

Thinking this couldn't be good I sat up and clutched the covers to my chest, while listening intently for more information.

Amos stood from the bed, gripping the phone in his hands. "Don't touch anything. Give me a few minutes to get dressed." He threw the phone down on the bed in a huff. "Briana said someone was killed."

I sucked in a breath and choked out, "Killed?" I turned to climb out of bed. "In the house? Who? How?"

Amos reached for the same pair of pants that he'd climbed into earlier. "She found a body in the shed."

"In the shed? I'm going with you."

He blew out a breath. "Eugeena, I can handle this. You don't need to go over there."

"Of course I do. When Leesa was in trouble, you helped me. Don't forget about Carmen and her friend, Jocelyn."

He rubbed his hand across his bald head.

I held up my hands to ward off his protests. "I'm just going to support you. And Briana must be scared out of her mind."

It was the least I could do. Plus, I was feeling really bad about my feelings towards Briana. *Lord, I'm sorry for not being more understanding about Briana. The girl is begging for help in her own way.*

I couldn't replace her mother, but it was obvious that Briana had been on a downward destructive spiral since her mother died.

I prayed that she hadn't gone off the deep end.

Chapter 2

This was not my first dead body.

Though I never worked a homicide like Amos, I've managed to help solve a few murder cases. I wouldn't call it a hobby, but I have managed to find myself investigating how people died, one being my dear friend, Mary Fleming. I'd been estranged from my friend for a few years. That fateful day something led me to her home while I was out walking. Finding her body had changed me forever and placed a different perspective on my retired years than I imagined.

I pushed that memory back as I stood next to Amos. It was silent in the backyard, like all the creatures decided to become still. The only sound was next door where Porgy, the Corgi that I inherited from Mary, was throwing a fit at the backdoor that led out to our yard.

I tore my eyes away from the body to peer over at Amos's daughter. Despite tears running down Briana's face, she stood rigid, her arms wrapped around her body like a straitjacket. I was worried she was either going into shock or on the verge of a nervous breakdown.

"No one touch anything." Amos stated as he dialed 9-1-1.

I didn't want to look any more than I already had, but I found myself curiously viewing the body in the shed again. I covered my nose, but could still smell the unpleasant odor of decay in the air. The woman's large brown eyes seemed to stare at something across from her. It wasn't her stillness that struck me as much as the large gash on the right side of her head.

Had she fallen somewhere? Or did someone hit her across the head with something?

Even more disturbing were the markings of dirt across the concrete floor. She'd been dragged into the shed and purposely placed across from the entrance, to be found by whoever walked through the door.

But, why?

And, who was she?

I had a sense that I'd seen the woman before. She appeared young, between the age of my daughter and Briana. Her clothing was casual, blue denim jeans, a bright yellow halter top and sandals. I could tell she'd artfully applied her makeup, though now the mascara was smeared across her cheeks. She was a really pretty woman with pecan colored skin, now lifeless. I wondered if I had her as a student. It was quite possible since I taught eighth grade social studies for so many years. It was a common occurrence for me to run into a former student, now an adult.

Something on her hand caught my attention. It appeared to be smudged from my distance. I pointed, "What's on her hand? That doesn't look like a tattoo."

Amos answered, "Looks like some kind of stamp. She may have been someplace else before arriving here."

I stepped back, suddenly feeling nauseous. The smell was waning my curiosity. This woman had been here for more than a few hours. I moved away from the door and farther into the yard. Amos followed suit a few seconds later. He stood by Briana as he gazed intently towards the shed.

Despite being a retired homicide detective, I'd learned that Amos couldn't turn down an investigation. This one tonight had hit too close to home.

I faced Briana whose body was turned towards the house like she wanted to flee at any moment.

I leaned in close and spoke softly, as if to a young child. "I don't know why, but she looks so familiar to me. Did you know her, Briana?"

Briana seemed to shrink inwardly, puzzlement on her face. "I don't know where she came from or why she was here."

During that instance, I noticed Briana had alcohol on her breath. She was standing upright, so she wasn't drunk, but she'd been drinking. I wanted to scold Briana. *What is wrong with you?* An even more important question, why was Briana letting all kinds of people in her father's house anyway? She was old enough to know better than to be this reckless. I glanced over at Amos. My husband's face reflected what I was thinking.

Amos peered over at his daughter, disapproval marred his face. He pointed towards the shed, "I'm pretty sure when CSI arrives they're not going to find a lot of blood inside the shed. That crime scene is somewhere else, maybe on this property." He paced the length of the yard by the shed. "Someone purposely chose to hide her body. That same person could have pushed her or possibly struck her with an object to cause that head damage." He peered around the yard as though searching for the murder weapon.

It took me a moment to process that information. My body began to shiver. "I can't believe someone would just leave her that way."

"Nothing surprises me anymore. I've seen it all. I have to say *this* on my property is a new one." Amos waved his arms. "Let's move inside the house. We've trampled around enough back here. Briana, you're going to have to answer some questions starting with who you invited into this house."

Briana stared back at her father, shaking her head. Her voice pitched higher than usual as she protested, "I don't know who would have done this. I don't even remember anyone being outside in the backyard or near the shed."

Amos grabbed her shoulders as though to keep her from flying off the handle. "I can hear the cops approaching. They just need to know who was here to start the investigation." He glanced over at me.

I arched an eyebrow. I felt pretty sure Amos was going to be doing some investigating on his own and he knew me. I was not about to let him leave me out.

As Amos predicted, blue lights and sirens arrived in front of the house. I had a feeling I knew who else from Charleston P.D. would show up soon. I had so many run-ins with the homicide detective, she knew me by name. I even had the detective's information in my phone contacts. A strange thing, but last fall I was pulled into a murder investigation as a civilian.

People like to confess things to me. I don't know why. Maybe it was because I'd been a teacher. I'd always had students who liked to confide in me.

Now, I have a homicide detective on speed dial.

The doorbell rang soon after we re-entered the house through the backdoor. I couldn't help but look around and notice Amos's former home in disarray. It was clear that Briana had a group of people in the house, especially in the kitchen. Dishes were in the sink, pizza and chicken wing boxes were stacked on the kitchen table, and I noticed quite a few beer cans and brown bottles spilling over the top of the trashcan. I wanted to immediately clean-up, but that wouldn't be a good idea. I headed into the living room behind Amos and Briana; this room appeared to be a disaster area too.

Pillows from the couch were piled in the corner and most of the dining room chairs were placed around the room indicating where people had sat while they visited.

Amos let the deputy in. Instead of sitting down, we all stood in the living room facing the young man who came to take our statement.

He glanced around briefly and then cleared his throat. "Someone reported a body."

Briana looked over at her father, seeming unsure how to answer.

Amos nodded. "Yes, my daughter called me. My wife and I live next door. We came right over and once I saw the body, I called 9-1-1. I'm a retired homicide detective."

The deputy frowned. "Okay, sir. Well, I assumed no one touched the body."

Briana shook her head vehemently. "No, as soon as I saw... I ran back into the house to call my dad."

The deputy had removed a notebook from his uniform's breast pocket. He flipped it open and clicked the pen in his hand. "Ma'am, did you recognize the person?"

Briana seemed to freeze for a moment before answering. "I don't think I knew her." She glanced over at her dad. "I mean she wasn't here with the others."

The deputy asked sharply, "Others?"

"I had a small get together last night and tonight. Most of the same people. Tonight, everyone had just left, most of them had jobs to get to in the morning. I was getting ready to take the trash out, but then I noticed the shed was open. I don't know why this caught my attention. I guess I wasn't sure if anyone was in there so I went to check. Then, I noticed a smell."

A frowned crossed the deputy's face. "Ma'am, how many people were here at the house this weekend? We're going to need all their names."

Briana stuttered, "I will try, but..."

My mouth spilled the question before I could help myself. "You don't know who all was in here, do you?"

She glared at me. "I knew most of them. Some people brought guests. That's normal. It wasn't more than fifteen or sixteen people."

I glanced over at Amos, whose forehead was wrinkled as if he was trying to ward off a pending headache.

"Just sit tight." The deputy held up his hands. "I'm going to secure the crime scene. The detective should be here any minute. If I was you, I would start jotting down names of those who were on the premises this evening."

Amos stood, "I can show you the way, deputy."

Amos and the deputy left the living room leaving me standing next to Briana.

I puzzled over her answers to the deputy's questions. Briana claimed she wasn't sure if she knew the woman, but I thought I sensed recognition in her eyes. Even I thought the woman looked familiar. I started to question Briana about her reaction, but the doorbell rang. I had a pretty good idea who it was before I headed towards the door.

"Let me get the door for you. I have had some run-ins with this Charleston homicide detective. Be on guard, because she doesn't play with her questions."

When I opened the door I was greeted by a petite redhead woman who by now I could have called a friend. But we didn't have that kind of relationship. Detective Sarah Wilkes didn't appear very pleased to see me and I kind of expected that. I did have a history which involved me butting into her investigations.

Still I knew she respected me and I knew she certainly respected Amos. Wilkes' father and Amos served together on the force, so they had a long history together.

She smiled, "Mrs. Patterson. Or should I call you Mrs. Jones now?"

I returned a smile, "I'm Mrs. Patterson-Jones now, but you know you're welcome to call me Eugeena."

Detective Wilkes nodded. "Miss Eugeena. Congratulations on your nuptials. I'm sorry I couldn't make the wedding, but you know in the back of my mind I figured you and I would meet again." She stepped into the house, a grimace on her face as she glanced around. "Here we are meeting again at another crime scene."

I frowned, "I hope you know I don't look for these crime scenes."

"No, they seem to find you." Detective Wilkes whipped out her notebook from inside her jacket pocket. "Who found the body?"

"I did." Briana crossed her arms, looking warily at Detective Wilkes.

The detective eyed the young woman. "You are?"

"Briana Jones. Amos is my father."

Detective Wilkes responded, "Uh-huh. Did you recognize the body?"

Briana seemed to freeze again before answering. Her response was low. "I don't think so."

I eyed Briana and then glanced over at the detective. Wilkes was watching Briana closely.

She picked up on it too. Briana had a definite reaction when she was asked that question. Did she know the dead woman outside? If so, how?

This was not going to go well if Briana was hiding something.

Chapter 3

The CSI unit arrived early Monday morning and stayed for hours marking various areas of Amos's property. At some point we ventured back over to our house. Despite the body being outside, Briana insisted she didn't want to be alone, so I set her up in one of the guest bedrooms downstairs. Eventually Amos and I climbed the stairs to our bedroom, but I tossed and turned as much as he did. After what felt like a really short night, I climbed out of bed, washed my face and brushed my teeth.

Porgy watched me from his doggy bed in the corner of our bedroom. Usually Amos was up before me and he let Porgy outside in the morning while I slept. I didn't want to disturb Amos, so I ushered the dog out of the bedroom with me. As much as his short legs allowed, the dog galloped down the stairs and then proceeded to bounce around my ankles to be let out the backdoor. As Porgy did his business outside in the yard, I started the coffee and took out some turkey bacon to begin breakfast. All the while I moved in the kitchen, I couldn't help but feel a weird sense of doom.

There was a body right next door. Again.

Last time this happened, Amos and I were together

when we heard gunshots. We ran out to find my next door neighbor's son shot dead in the doorway of the house. We clearly heard the gunshot and saw the driver take off down the road. Sometime last night or even yesterday, someone placed that woman's body inside the shed.

My question. Was this to get Briana or Amos's attention?

Amos arrived in the kitchen looking like he could have used more sleep. He headed to the backdoor and let Porgy back in.

After pouring Amos a cup of coffee, I asked, "Did anyone identify the woman last night? I feel like I knew her from somewhere."

He shook his head and took a slurp of coffee. "No, but I expect she will be identified soon. I just don't know how or why someone would put her in the shed." He took a deep breath, "Were they trying to pin this on Briana? Doesn't make sense. She just came back to South Carolina three months ago."

As I pulled eggs out of the refrigerator, it struck me that Amos had no doubts of any involvement by Briana with this woman's death. Of course, I didn't think Briana did anything either. She had a sharp tongue and fierce attitude, but she was a sensitive soul. Maybe it was her sensitivity or just the shock that made Briana appear like she had something to hide last night.

Besides, another theory had been troubling me, and I didn't really want to voice it out loud. However, given Amos's former profession and my obsession with watching crime shows, I had no choice. "Amos, do you think someone from your past could be messing with you? You haven't been out of that house that long. Maybe someone found your address and didn't know you had moved out."

He raised a bushy eyebrow, "That crossed my mind too, but I didn't recognize the woman either. This morning when Briana gets up, I want to know who was in that house this past weekend."

I cracked the eggs in a bowl, added pepper and then whisked the eggs. As I scrambled the eggs, I thought about the fact that I never saw the people that showed up over at the house with Briana. Usually they arrived after Amos and I had retired for the night. It struck me that with Briana just being back a few months in Sugar Creek, there couldn't be that many people she still knew. I knew Amos's girls graduated from the same high school my children attended, but I didn't know the family that well back then. We were both married to different spouses and Amos didn't move into this neighborhood until after his girls had graduated.

In a lot of ways, I didn't know either of his daughters. Briana was especially difficult to get to know because she still grieved her mother and her relationship with Amos was still on rocky ground.

I scooped the scrambled eggs on the plates. I wasn't sure when Briana would get up, but I was fairly sure it wouldn't be any time soon. She wasn't a morning person. Despite being retired, most days I still kept the same schedule I had as a school teacher. I arose early and started my day even if I didn't have much on my to do list.

As Amos and I consumed breakfast, I pondered how to ask Amos questions about his daughter. I decided to start with her life before her mom's death and before she left South Carolina. "So, since Briana's been back has she been mainly connecting with friends from high school?"

Amos grunted as he shoveled eggs and bacon into his mouth. "She's been seeing a guy she used to date. I didn't like him back then. I noticed he was there Saturday night when I went to talk to Briana. He was a big guy back then. Seemed even bigger now. If Briana wasn't throwing such a fit, I would have asked him to leave."

I frowned, "What's his name? I'm telling you, if he grew up around here, I probably had him in eighth grade."

Amos grinned, "You remember all your students."

I shrugged, "Not all of them, but the more memorable characters I definitely haven't forgotten."

Amos nodded. "That makes sense. My line of work was like that. Some folks you don't forget." He pushed his empty plate away from him. "This guy's name is Theo Nichols."

My eyes widened at the name. "Theo Nichols. Yes, I knew him and his brother, Damion. Theo was the eldest; he had a temper, but he was able to pour his energy into sports. He ended up doing pretty well with football, played for South Carolina State. Damion was a year younger, always managing to get into trouble. I remember he had the body for football, but not the discipline. Don't they own the auto detailing shop downtown?"

Amos nodded, "Yep, that's their shop. Briana was crazy about Theo. I mean I could see why, he was the typical popular jock. There was something about him though, no matter how much he excelled on the field, he felt like bad news to me. Girls like their bad boys! I don't know if he was there last night or not, but he is one of those people I wouldn't put past trying to hurt someone."

I sighed, "Someone dragged the woman into the shed trying to hide her. What was the point? And you know what, I had another thought that seems ludicrous. Suppose she wasn't killed in your yard at all. I've seen enough shows on television where someone calls themselves getting rid of a body. But like that. That's obviously trying to set someone up for the crime."

"You're right about that. It will take the lab some time but hopefully they can find some forensics. Once they identify her, they can start creating a timeline of the woman's actions the past week. Preferably they can do it soon."

There was something else bothering me, but I wasn't sure if I should bring it up. Amos got along great with my two sons and daughter. They accepted him beautifully and I think that was largely because Amos and I didn't move that fast. We started as friends and gradually he just became a part of my life. Amos has always reached out to my sons letting them know he respected them as men and he's been there for Leesa and her kids.

I didn't want to do anything to step over the line with his girls. I knew how important it was to him to have them back in his life.

Before I could ask him anything else, Briana showed up at the kitchen door. She looked like she hadn't slept. She eyed Porgy who had been laying in the corner of the kitchen in his bed. My doggie lifted his head and barked. Porgy was not much of a barker. Really, he only barked at people that he didn't like and for whatever reason my dog didn't like Briana.

Porgy, I'm suspicious too. Briana was hiding something. I just knew it.

In fact, her sudden appearance and determination to stay in Sugar Creek had me on alert.

Chapter 4

I prayed over my attitude towards Briana. I really didn't know why my suspicions popped up like they did. I was not one to question my gut feelings, but I knew I needed to set aside my suspicions. She seemed to still be in shock and hadn't rested at all. I couldn't blame her. There was no rest for one who laid eyes on a human, knowing they died a horrible death.

I inquired, "How are you doing this morning, Briana? I hope you were able to get some sleep."

She grimaced, "No, unfortunately I couldn't."

Amos waved his daughter over to the table. "Come on over and have some breakfast. Don't worry, we will get to the bottom of what happened to that woman."

Looking unsure, Briana sat down next to her father. "What do you mean we? Aren't the police going to handle this?"

I frowned, "Your dad isn't going to let this go even if he is retired."

Amos nodded, "This isn't going away, especially once they identify the woman. We need to know what happened."

I took out more eggs and prepared to scramble them. As

I cooked, I kept an ear cocked for the conversation that I felt should be addressed.

I knew Amos was concerned it could have been one of his old cases, but that theory didn't feel right to me. Why now? Amos had been living at that house for some time. Why would they leave a body once he moved out? I knew Amos's former profession made him run into all kinds of criminals, but I'd never until this moment thought his past life would affect us.

I scooped the eggs onto a plate and passed them to Briana.

She mumbled, "Thanks."

As I watched her eat, I thought, *At least her appetite is still good.* The peace of the moment over breakfast would surely not last.

Briana seemed to come awake after finishing her food. "Dad, do I need a lawyer?"

Amos raised his eyebrow, "You didn't do anything wrong."

"No, but I can tell that detective was suspicious of me last night. She asked all these questions as though I put ... *that body* in the shed."

Amos sighed, "Well, somebody did. We need that list of people you gave the detective."

Briana sat up, "Why?"

"So we can stay ahead of the police. I need to know who you let into the house."

Briana crossed her arms. "They were good people."

I rolled my eyes. "You were by yourself most of the day yesterday. Did you happen to be outside in the yard?"

Briana bristled at my voice. "I didn't kill anyone and stuff them in the shed."

Amos barked, "Eugeena is not accusing you of

anything. She's asking a question that makes sense. Did you notice anything different yesterday? Were you in the shed?"

I added, "I'm not expert on this kind of stuff like your dad, but I watch enough TV shows to know. You have to know your timeline to support an alibi. Detective Wilkes can't accuse you of anything as long as you can account for your whereabouts."

Briana seemed to grow smaller in the chair. She crossed her arms as though she was feigning away cold air. "You're right. I'm sorry. This has me all messed up in the head. I didn't sleep at all. All I could see was ... that woman's face." She swallowed. "She definitely wasn't there before folks started coming over. I did go to the shed on Friday because I remembered the lawn chairs were in there." She wrinkled her forehead in concentration. "I wasn't in the yard at all yesterday."

Amos shook his head. "So someone could have placed the body in the shed in the past twenty-four hours. You didn't have anyone over on Friday?"

Briana squirmed in her seat. "Just one person."

I tried not to raise my eyebrow, but it shot up anyway. I had a feeling I knew the identity of the one person based on my earlier conversation with Amos.

He cleared his throat, avoiding the subject of who. "I'm trying to get some information from some associates who still work on the force. As soon as the body is identified, then we can start figuring out what happened to her."

I took a swig from my mug, the coffee had grown cold. "I still feel like I know her from someplace." I looked at my phone, noting the time. "I need to get to the church soon for summer camp."

Nothing went unnoticed in our neighborhood, Sugar

Creek. Someone knew or saw something and I knew just where to start.

Chapter 5

The scent of hot dogs met me at the door indicating my favorite people had arrived at Missionary Baptist Church before me. Annie Mae Brown and Willie Mae Brown were not my closest friends, but they made my life, well, interesting. Both women still could carry on something awful, stirring up unnecessary trouble. But life had struck them a bad blow and it seemed to have mellowed both of them. Willie Mae lost her daughter tragically a year ago and she was not the same woman. We were all the same age, but Willie Mae appeared to have gained ten years with her hair going completely white compared to her twin. Of course, I suspected Annie Mae was still sneaking the box of black hair dye.

Jet black. Yeah, right! I'm sorry but when a woman gets a certain age she should be proud of those strands of gray. The Bible said that's a sign of wisdom. Who doesn't want wisdom?

As I stepped further inside the fellowship hall, the twins watched me. Well, sort of. I don't care how many years I'd known the woman, Willie Mae's wandering eye still threw me off. Her eye never quite focused on your face and seemed to concentrate on something far off. Which made me want to turn my head to see what was over my shoulders.

I felt bad every single time. This time I stopped myself from the urge and stared her in the face. Now we could have faced off like that for a while but we had children arriving any moment for the camp. Besides, I wanted to know what these two busybodies saw last night.

Willie Mae stated, "We saw the cops were over at Amos's old place last night."

These sisters never disappoint!

I tried to keep the smile off my face as I continued past them to place my bag behind the counter in the kitchen. That was Sugar Creek. People knew your business, sometimes before you knew yourself. I faced them both, "Hello, ladies. I guess those flashing lights caught your attention."

Annie Mae piped up, "The cops were there all night. Did I see the coroner too?"

"Unfortunately, yes." There was no need to try to shut this conversation down. It was bound to be reported on the news soon. Still I was hesitant to share Amos's business with these two. Who knew which way the story would be transformed by the time they shared the events from last night with other church members.

I straightened my shoulders, hoping my trust wouldn't blow up in my face later once the rumor wheel started turning. "Briana came across a young woman who... well, she'd been killed."

Both twins clutched their hearts in unison like they were about to have a Fred Sanford moment. The twins spilled out their dismay together. "What's going on?" "People are getting killed in our neighborhood all the time."

I balked, "People are not getting killed all the time. Now there are a lot of us dropping like flies due to poor health and old age." I counted on my fingers quickly. "The body last night made three deaths that were clearly violent in the past few years."

"Violent." Willie Mae scoffed, "Do you know who the woman was?"

I grimaced, "No, but the funny thing is I felt like I've seen her before."

Annie Mae leaned in closer as if she needed to examine my head. "You saw the body?"

"Yes, Briana was frantic and not sure what to do. Amos went over to the house and I followed."

Annie frowned, "What did Briana do?"

I sighed, "She didn't do anything but find a body."

Annie Mae inquired, "How did it get there?"

I shot back, "Good question. We have no idea, but we do want to find out who this woman was and who would do this."

Willie Mae harrumphed, "There have been all kinds of people going in and out of that house."

I eyed her. "And you know this because..."

She threw her hands up. "I watch the house. Shouldn't you be doing the same? You are still the head of neighborhood watch, aren't you?"

That made me wince. Willie Mae had a point. Since Amos moved in, my interests had been preoccupied with being married again. I love Amos, but it took some time adjusting the house and my mind to sharing a home with someone again. One wouldn't think living alone for five years would make such a big difference in your mindset. I mean I was complaining about being lonely!

I still didn't know how I got stuck with chairing the

neighborhood watch. I tried, but had been unsuccessful with passing this task along to someone else. Everyone wanted to be nosy but not in charge. Go figure!

I snapped back and realized Wille Mae was still ranting. "The music is so loud! And at night when folks are trying to get some sleep. I wanted to see who was over there and if I had to call somebody's mama."

"Ha!" Now that cracked me up. "Those were grown people not children."

Annie Mae shook her head, "Some grown people never grow up."

I had to agree. There was no way I could defend Briana, especially since Amos and I had some sleepless nights too. I felt really bad that the Brown sisters had been disturbed. Goodness, they lived three houses down. Which made me wonder exactly how Willie Mae was doing her snooping. Did the woman have binoculars?

I wanted to ask her who she saw, but couldn't discuss the neighborhood troubles anymore since a few of the children along with more adult volunteers were entering the fellowship hall. The twins went back to setting up plates on the table. I greeted the children as they signed in for the day, grabbed name tags and then headed for the snack table. We'd been offering the summer camp for four weeks now, taking a break last week for the Fourth of July holiday. We had two more weeks to go. Today was designated craft day. Thankfully, we took time after Sunday School yesterday to set out the materials for the various age groups in each classroom.

Usually I would take on the pre-teens, which was the age I taught most of my years as a school teacher, but we didn't have any from that age range to sign-up for summer camp this year. The Brown sisters handled kindergarten through second grade, while I worked with third through fifth grade students. One of my camp students, Amani Gladstone, was a regular from our after school program. As her customary greeting, she came running towards me and gave me a big hug. Amani was the granddaughter of one of my high school classmates, so I've watched Amani and her mom grow up.

"How are you today, Amani? I know you have a birthday coming up soon."

Amani smiled, "I'm doing good. I'm glad we have camp this week. It was really boring last week at home. I miss being at school."

I grinned, "I imagine that you do. Your grandmother told me you did really good in school. All A's this time."

"Yes, ma'am." Suddenly looking serious, Amani glanced around. Then she leaned in and whispered. "Ms. Eugeena, there's a lady sitting outside in her car. She looked like she was crying."

I leaned in toward Amani. I'd found she was an observant little girl, sometimes noticing things she shouldn't. "Is she in the church parking lot outside?"

Amani nodded, her eyes wide.

"Okay, I'm going to go over to the window and look out. Do you remember what color her car was?"

"Yes, ma'am. It's blue. I remember that color. Blue is one of my favorite colors."

I patted the little girl on her shoulder. "Why don't you head back to the classroom and I will check on the lady?"

I watched as Amani went to the back of the class before peeking out the window. I couldn't see the car in question so I decided to head outside. It may have been nothing, but I didn't want to take any chances of a stranger being on the property.

As soon as I stepped outside, whoever was in the car slung the driver's door open. The vehicle appeared to be a blue Nissan Altima. In fact, for a split second, I thought it was my daughter's car, but the blue wasn't the right shade. An older woman with disheveled hair climbed out and approached the doorway where I stood.

The closer she got, the more her facial features came into focus. *That's Gladys Howell.* She hadn't been attending Missionary Baptist regularly. In fact, she was part of a group who had a falling out when the young pastor took over for his father. Something silly about Pastor Jones being too young and doing too much.

Church folk!

Lately, I noticed Gladys had started attending services again.

Gladys stopped in front of me, almost tipping over her heavy chested body. "Oh, Eugeena. It's so good to see you. It's been a long time."

I held out my arms because I didn't want the woman tipping over on me. Neither one of us could afford a hip injury. "Yes, it has. I've been seeing you the past few Sundays, but haven't had a moment to talk. How are the grandchildren?"

Gladys appeared to be trying to catch her breath. "They're doing good. I dropped them off today. One of the Brown sisters let me register them yesterday."

"Oh, I should have known that." I touched her shoulder, "Gladys, are you okay?"

She held her hands over her head, her face scrunched into the beginnings of an ugly cry. "No. You remember my daughter Sondra?"

Some days my memory wasn't too good, but I nodded.

"I haven't seen Sondra in two days. That isn't like her.

She works two jobs now, but she loves her kids. I've never known her to stay away this long. Anyway, I was hoping the pastor was here. I wanted to see if he could pray with me."

The more I looked at Gladys's distraught face, the more another face appeared in my mind. Something struck me in that moment of clarity, and a chill traveled down my spine with such a quickness I shivered despite it being July and well over ninety degrees outside.

Last night's events spiraled in my head and I knew without a doubt my onset fright was a bad sign.

Chapter 6

I didn't want to have this conversation outside in front of the church. "Unfortunately, Pastor Jones is visiting with homebound members. He may or may not swing by the office today. Why don't we come inside out of the heat? You can tell me what happened and when you last saw Sondra."

As I led Gladys inside, we walked past the fellowship hall where the children had gathered for a snack. Annie Mae looked up to see us walking by. I shook my head at her inquisitive look and led Gladys further down the hall to one of the adult Sunday School classrooms.

I had no idea why I remembered Sondra Howell during our walk. I pictured a younger version of her in my mind when she was in my class. It's amazing how I could recall a student from my classroom from fourteen years ago out of the blue. Sondra was a smart girl. She also had a really smart mouth too. But she loved learning and talking about history. She was also one of those students who retained information easily without a lot of study. I remembered her doing well on her exams, scoring high grades.

Gladys sat down heavily in one of the chairs, while I closed the door behind us. I didn't want prying ears and hoped the children kept the Brown sisters preoccupied. I pulled up a chair next to Gladys.

"How has Sondra been doing?"

Gladys seemed taken aback by my question. "What do you mean?"

"Was she doing okay the last time you saw her? Happy? Sad?"

Glady shrugged. "Sondra has some awful mood swings sometimes. Saturday night, she went out with some friends and seemed to be in a better mood than usual."

"I see. I'm so sorry you are going through this; I want you to know I understand perfectly what you're going through. My Leesa ran off and left her kids with me for a few days. After birthing her second child, she was totally overwhelmed at the time and needed a break. I had no idea where she was, worried me silly, but she returned a few days later."

I sat back in the chair, "I remember Sondra being an excellent student, but it's hard to keep up with children after they leave my classroom. I know she graduated from high school because the church presented her with a plaque during her graduation year."

Gladys sighed. "I hate to say it, but it's been hard to get her to come to church since she's been an adult. She had her first child not too long after she graduated. Things were fine for a while, but she had trouble keeping a job. Then, she had another child. Since she had the second one, she's been trying to be more stable. Now she works all the time. I hardly see her some days. Her and the children moved back in with me a few years ago."

I nodded. Sondra sounded pretty similar to my Leesa in a lot more ways than I expected. "Did Sondra say where she was going?"

Gladys wrung her hands, "No. She had the day off on Saturday. Which was really unusual, she always worked weekends." The woman swallowed, trying to catch her breath as she spilled out the story. "I thought she would spend the day with the kids, but she slept most of the day. I didn't hear a peep from her until late in the day. When she does that, kind of hide in her room, I know she's in a bad mood about something. The last thing I wanted to do was argue with her. I let her be and made sure the kids stayed out of her way. That night she walked out of the room, dressed and ready to go."

My mind thought back to the outfit the woman wore in the shed. I envisioned the bright yellow halter top, sure to have turned heads. I shook the memory away and murmured, "Sounds like she was tired and ready to let off some steam."

Gladys frowned, "Yeah, it's the new job. She works during the day at the Food Lion. A few months ago, she'd started working at the Black Diamond Night Club. I wasn't happy about her being out at night in that atmosphere, but she claimed she made good money."

"What does she do there?"

"Waitressing. That's always been her thing before she started working as a cashier. I didn't think she ever wanted to go back but she claims the tips she receives are good. Even talked about quitting her job at Food Lion."

"Have you reached out to any of Sondra's friends since Saturday?"

Gladys shook her head. "She used to hang out with Charlene Hunt when they were young, but the past few years they haven't really been speaking. I know someone picked her up outside, but I didn't get a chance to see who it was. I was busy trying to get the kids settled in for the night."

"Women have fallings out all the time. Do you know why she may have stopped talking to Charlene?"

Gladys closed her eyes.

"Gladys, are you okay?"

Her eyes flipped open, filled with tears. "A lot of people stopped hanging around Sondra because of *that* man. I can't even refer to him as a man, but he's the father of my grandbabies. He certainly is choosy when he sees them and when he decides to take care of him."

"Did Sondra have trouble with him?"

"Nothing but trouble with *that* one."

"Have you reached out to him to ask if he's seen Sondra?"

"Yes, in fact that's where I was coming from when I saw the church. That man made me so angry. He acted like he didn't care about the mother of his children being missing. He told me I was being a drama queen and that she would probably show up any time. He made my nerves so bad, I had to swing by here and talk to Pastor Jones."

"I'm sorry he isn't here."

"Not a problem, I appreciate you listening to me."

"I'm here to be supportive where I can. I hate to ask so many questions, but I'm concerned. Have you reached out to the police at all? I know she's an adult, but you can report her as a missing person."

Gladys nodded. "That will be my next stop."

"Good, they will want a current photo of Sondra. Do you have one?"

"Yes, I do. In fact, she insisted that her daughter take a photo of her Saturday night." Gladys pulled her phone out of her bag.

I watched as she slid her fingers across the phone, dread returning to my mind. I suddenly was afraid of my reaction to what Gladys had on her phone. She swiped a number of times until she found the photo she wanted. She turned the phone around to me. "How about this one? Do you think this will work? She's wearing the clothes she had on that night."

I stared at the photo for a long uncomfortable few seconds before answering. "Yes, that photo should do fine. You should get to the police station as soon as possible."

I walked Gladys out into the hallway where we met Pastor Jones arriving.

"Hello, ladies. How are you doing this fine day?"

I responded in Gladys's place, "Pastor Jones, good to see you today. Ms. Howell really needs your help." I wanted to pass Gladys off to the pastor quickly because now I had a mission. I needed to call Amos and find out what to do about what I'd just found out.

I was pretty sure the woman in the shed last night was Sondra Howell. I had no idea how she got there and why, but now I was more determined to find out.

Chapter 7

The entire time I drove, I berated myself for not recognizing the woman right away. Okay, it had been a number of years, but still I really did know her. She was one of my students. Now I knew she was perfectly fine Saturday night. What happened in twenty-four hours? Was Sondra on Amos's property sometime Saturday or Sunday night? So much about this murder bothered me.

When I arrived home, Amos's truck was in the driveway. I was anxious to find out any information he'd obtained today. Once inside, I noticed it was quiet. The television in the living room was not on. I called out, "Amos."

I walked down the hall and noticed the guest bedroom door was closed. When I passed by the closed bedroom door, I thought I heard something or someone. I paused and stepped up close to the door. Was Briana crying?

I started to tap on the door, but then heard the backdoor open. Porgy's yips could be heard clear down the hallway. That dog must have sensed I was home because next thing I knew he was tearing around the corner towards me. I couldn't help but smile.

Amos was in the kitchen washing his hands at the sink.

I glanced out the kitchen window and noticed the riding lawn mower was in the middle of the yard. "I see you've been busy out in the yard."

"Yes, I needed something to keep me busy."

"You mean from checking out the crime scene," I winked at him.

He smiled, "That too."

I grabbed some glasses from the cabinet and then reached inside the fridge. "Did you get any info about the case?" After filling each glass with ice cubes from the icemaker, I poured some ice tea as Amos settled at the kitchen table.

He cocked his eyebrow. "Nope. Any contacts I have at the station were not cooperating today. I kept getting warned away."

I swirled the ice around in my tea before taking a long sip. "Why do you think your cop friends are being hush-hush on this one?"

Amos took a long drink from his glass before responding. The frown marks in his large forehead seemed to be even deeper. "Probably because the body was in my yard. Or, well, in the backyard of a house I own. I'm sure Detective Wilkes is making it known that she wants no interference with the case." He sighed deeply, "Briana didn't make it any better. She didn't cooperate last night."

I sat up in my chair. I still felt like Briana was hiding something, but didn't want to come out and say so. "Maybe she was still in shock."

"Maybe."

"I'm still in shock myself." I told him about Gladys Howell's visit to the church today and mentioning she was looking for her daughter. "I had a strange feeling. I felt so bad that I didn't remember the girl until her mom started talking. I was kind of ashamed because I knew her face looked familiar last night."

"Wait," Amos held up his hand. "How do you know the woman in the shed was Sondra?"

"I mentioned to Gladys that she might want to report Sondra missing to the police and to be sure to have a current photo. She had a picture in her phone of her the other night. Amos, it was her! Same clothes."

He shook his head. "If I had known you were going to find out that fast, I wouldn't have bothered my boys today."

I knew by *boys* that Amos was referring to fellow retirees, his former partner, Joe Douglas, and another colleague, Lenny Wilkes. Wilkes happened to be the father of our infamous Detective Sarah Wilkes. Both Joe and Lenny headed up their own private detective agency and occasionally sent work to Amos when he was interested.

I smacked his arm. "Believe me it was purely a divine setup. Amani just happened to tell me someone was outside crying. I went to check and this woman fell in my lap, literally since Pastor Jones wasn't around. I figured you would reach out to Joe and Lenny for this."

He drained his glass of tea and leaned back in the kitchen chair. "Yeah. The one piece of information Joe was able to gather intel on was the symbol on her right hand." He reached in his shirt pocket and pulled out a notebook, probably similar to the one issued to him when he was a cop. He pointed to a symbol on a piece of paper.

It looked like a diamond now that I saw it up close.

Amos continued, "There wasn't any ID on her, but this was probably a stamp from a nightclub. That fits with what her mother said about her going out Saturday evening.

Detective Wilkes will probably narrow down which nightclub and show a photo around. Did you mention anything about last night to Gladys?"

"No, I was scared too. I didn't want that kind of news coming from me. Should I say something, as a lead to Detective Wilkes? I don't want to be accused of meddling!"

"No, it's good you didn't. Wilkes will find out soon enough as long as Gladys goes to the police."

"I'm sure she will. I can check back with her tomorrow." I perked up, "You know what, apparently one of Sondra's jobs was working at the Black Diamond Night Club. Would Sondra go and hang out at the place where she worked?"

Amos shrugged, "It's quite possible, especially if employees get discounts. It would be easy to look for the club and see if this symbol is used there."

"Then what?"

Amos answered, "It would be great to find out who was around Sondra that night."

I shook my head, "Gladys did mention that Sondra had an on and off again relationship with her kids' father. You know I didn't get his name. Suppose he had something to do with it?"

"Oftentimes domestic violence turns into foul play. It's quite possible Sondra could have had a fatal run-in with this boyfriend. In fact, I can see that scenario of a boyfriend hiding the body."

"Well, I can certainly reach out to Gladys and get a name. When do you think this will all be confirmed by the police? I was so nervous talking to her today knowing about last night's discovery."

"Knowing Detective Wilkes, she's probably already

identified Sondra and mapped out the timeline. It's a matter of rounding up suspects."

I wrung my hands. "I can't believe it was Sondra Howell. I remember her at thirteen having a lethal mouth. She was not afraid to speak what was on her mind no matter the consequences. In fact, she got on my nerves a couple of times. She was one of those children who liked to talk back to adults." I sighed, "I wonder who she made angry enough to kill her?"

"Good question."

I know we didn't want to go there again, but I had to ask. "Have you been looking at your old cases? Any connections?"

Amos scratched his head. "Yeah, I talked to Joe. I'm checking on the status of some inmates that I had suspicions about, but I don't see anyone getting out of prison to come and pin a murder on me."

"Stranger things can happen. So will you keep looking?"

"Of course." He eyed me, "Are you worried?"

"No. Well, sort of. You know Annie Mae and Willie Mae were upset that we have had all these murders in our neighborhood. It's really not that many. But this murder is very different."

"It's disturbing and I don't blame the Brown sisters for being worried." He reached in his pocket again and unfolded a piece of paper. "Briana was reluctant to share this with me."

"The list?" I picked up the yellow sheet of paper that looked to be pulled from a legal pad. There were some names I immediately recognized and others I didn't. I counted about twenty names. I didn't even know Briana had that many people over at the house. One name in particular was missing. "This can't be everyone. Sondra's name isn't even on the list."

Amos shook his head, "I know, but it's a start. Someone on this list had to know Sondra. Maybe she showed up and Briana wasn't aware she was there. Either way, we need to know who did run into Sondra and were angry enough to not only strike her dead but attempt to hide the body on my property."

I heard movement at the kitchen door and looked up to see Briana's distraught face.

Amos turned to see his daughter. Frowning, he asked, "Briana, are you okay?"

I cocked an eyebrow thinking about what I'd learned about Sondra so far. Her and Briana had to be in the same age range. I asked, "Did you know Sondra Howell?"

Briana cringed as if someone had punched her in the chest, then turned and fled from the doorway. The next thing I comprehended was the front door slamming closed.

Amos and I stared at each other.

I finally stated what had been on my mind since last night. "Amos, I think Briana knows a lot more than she's told us or the police."

He closed his eyes, "I think so too. Eugeena, I don't know what to do. I'm fearful she's done something that I can't help her get out of this time."

This time.

What had Briana done before, and what did Amos have to do the last time?

Chapter 8

Briana never returned to the house and though I tried to move on with our evening, Amos's statement still bugged me. I became interested in Amos only two years ago. At the time, I couldn't understand why the man next door had caught my attention. Now here we were married a whole five months. Married life had been good, but we didn't know everything about each other's past lives. That was okay with us both being over sixty. We had entire lives with other people. Still, I didn't want us to be having secrets.

Secrets with ramifications.

Amos's statement had spun up my anxiety level. It had already been elevated since we discovered the body next door. Knowing the woman's identity made her death even more real.

I managed to grill some chicken breast and sauté some green beans. It wasn't a fancy meal, but it would do. I couldn't concentrate on cooking anything too complex while my mind spun up all kinds of foolishness. You know your mind does that to you sometimes, just let the imagination take over. I had to flat out say to myself, "Eugeena, stop it." This was Amos's daughter, and this man had been nothing but good to my children. Whatever Amos had done for his daughter before, it couldn't be that bad.

Me and the Lord knew how many nights I prayed over my children knowing they were up to no good and in some cases winded up in trouble, and they turned out just fine. *Praise the Lord!*

We ate dinner in silence, which was unusual. Amos and I usually had conversations about our day, the children, the grands and occasionally squabbled over local happenings and the news. I cleared the table, busying myself with loading the dishwasher. When I finished, I turned around and the list that Amos had pulled out earlier caught my eye. I grabbed the piece of paper and sat. "We didn't talk about this list. Do you know the people on this list?"

Amos had been typing on his phone. He'd been doing that a lot lately. Like me, he wasn't a tech geek, but somehow those little devices took over your life. I often caught Amos engrossed in a game, which I found funny. It seemed out of the ordinary for him.

"Amos," I repeated and waved the list at him.

He lifted his head and nodded, "Some of them. But only two names concern me."

I frowned. *So he did hear me when I asked the question before.*

He continued not paying any attention to my face, which spoke volumes. "I plan on meeting with one or both of them tomorrow."

Amos was going to have me developing wrinkles with the workout on my face. I could feel the tension in my forehead as my frown deepened. I guessed the two names he was referring to were at the top of the list. The Nichols boys, Theo and Damion.

"Is that really a good idea, Amos?"

He waved like it was no big deal. "Don't worry. I need some work done on my truck too. I have a cover story," he winked.

Amos might have been acting like this was no big deal, but I still didn't like the idea. He'd already let it be known he wasn't pleased with Theo visiting Briana the other night. What exactly was he planning to ask the brothers?

Did you kill a girl and leave her body in my shed?

I doubted seriously that a sixty-four year old man was going to make two young men confess. Young people rarely showed respect for their elders anyway. But before I could convey my concerns, Amos stood from the table. "I'm going to go next door to check on Briana."

"Okay, if you don't mind, my first thought would be to check out some of these names on Facebook."

The grin that crossed Amos's face almost made me blush.

He pointed his finger at me, "I knew you couldn't resist so don't let me stop you."

After doing some other cleaning touch-ups in the kitchen, I grabbed my laptop and settled on the couch in the living room. I usually spent time in the evenings playing around on Facebook anyway, so I had to force myself not to scroll through the feed. It took me a whole twenty minutes to pull myself from watching funny video after video. I needed the humor, and laughter is good medicine. Some of my anxiety from earlier disappeared. Finally getting down to business, I started typing in names from the list starting with the two guys.

The Nichols brothers had Facebook pages, but they

didn't post much. Some posts were from Instagram, mainly cars they worked on in their auto body shop. My preferred social media vice remained Facebook only. I still hadn't quite gotten the hang of Instagram, though Leesa talked me into creating an account. All I saw most days was a whole lot of selfies.

Speaking of selfies, the brothers did a lot of posing, looking more like overgrown teenagers than men. I had both of these young men in my classroom years ago, so I knew they were in their late twenties. Both brothers shared the same solemn look on their faces like it would hurt them to show some teeth. They were good-looking as boys and still remained handsome, now taller and more buffed than they were in my eighth grade class. I recalled Theo always being large for his age, while his younger brother, Damion, was small and skinny. He was only a year younger than Theo but it took him a while to catch up to his brother.

Theo was bald, which was surprising to me. I wondered if that was by choice or if he had already started prematurely losing his hair. His skin was milk-chocolate and he had the most expressive brown eyes which almost seemed to not fit his solemn face. There was a hint of dimples. If the man smiled, women would probably lose their minds over them.

Morris Chestnut. I snapped my fingers, Theo reminded me of him. I tickled myself sometimes at what I could recall. I may have been a history teacher, but I kept up on the pop culture stuff too.

I clicked on the younger brother's page. Damion resembled his older brother in bulk and height but had bright, caramel skin. Same expressive eyes as his brother's, but Damion's eyes were hazel and almost sorrowful like a puppy who'd lost his owner. In several photos, Damion wore his close-cut hair with blond streaks, reminding me of that singer Chris Brown.

These were indeed two good-looking men. With Briana just coming back to town a few months ago, I wondered how she hooked up with them. She certainly had no problem inviting them to the house. Maybe she'd kept in touch all these years.

Growing tired of looking at the Nichols boys, I scoured the list, recognizing a few other names who were all definitely students of mine. If people filled out their profiles on Facebook, an amateur detective like myself could gather quite a bit of data. I'd come to the conclusion that most of these people were in the same age range and probably were Sondra's classmates. These folks had known each other all their lives, attended the same schools and graduated together.

That started me thinking.

Though they didn't live in Sugar Creek while the girls were in school, Amos mentioned that Briana graduated from North Charleston high school. I knew when my own children had attended, the high school averaged six hundred students with about one hundred and fifty students per class.

Sondra and Briana had to have been aware of each other.

Why was Briana acting like she didn't recognize her?

I needed to know more about Sondra. I was still peeved at myself for not recognizing her. I could blame it on the state of her deceased body inside the shed. The horror of it all made me shiver slightly. I rubbed my arms, looking up from the laptop.

Focus, Eugeena. The Lord is my protector.

I didn't have time to be getting weirded out now. I shook myself and typed in Sondra's name. There were quite a few Sondra Howell Facebook pages and it took me some time to find the right page. Interesting enough, I found Sondra's page by surfing through my daughter's page. Apparently, Leesa and Sondra were friends on Facebook.

That surprised me because Leesa was younger. After further calculations in my tired head, I came to the conclusion that Leesa was probably a freshman when Sondra was a senior. Leesa told me once people just friended and followed each other on social media to have the numbers. Those relationships weren't always real. Still, I would be curious to know my daughter's take on Sondra.

As I perused the posts Sondra kept public, I noticed a pattern. Despite Gladys mentioning that Sondra didn't attend church, I found her page filled with bible verses, especially in the days prior to her death. I even spotted one of my favorites.

"Do not be anxious about anything, but in every situation, by prayer and petition, with thanksgiving, present your requests to God. And the peace of God, which transcends all understanding, will guard your heart and your mind in Christ Jesus" (Philippians 4:6-7, NIV).

As I scrolled down, I read another one from the book of John, "Do not let your heart be troubled. You believe in God; believe also in me" (John 14:1, NIV).

It seemed to me Sondra was going through something and she poured out her anguish on her Facebook page. I wondered if Sondra was suffering from some type of depression. She worked a lot, but Gladys said she spent the whole day in bed on Saturday, not really spending time with her children. She could have just been tired, but that was a little concerning to me. What was going through Sondra's mind? Did she just sleep the whole day from exhaustion or was something else bothering her?

Folks didn't often deal with mental illness. I knew this from experience. Leesa suffered from postpartum depression after delivering her second child. Previously, as a teenager, she grieved deeply from the loss of her best friend during her junior year in high school. Her grief led to a rebellious period that resulted in her first child and my first granddaughter, Keisha.

I decided to ramp up my nosiness and dug a little deeper into Sondra's photos, at least those that were public. She kept quite a few photos of her children on public view, which I thought wasn't a good idea. As I looked at Sondra's little boy and girl, I recalled seeing both children in summer camp at Missionary Baptist this morning, specifically in Annie Mae's class. I'd never made the connection they were Sondra's kids. We had a lot of children attending the church's summer camp who resided in the nearby community and needed a place to be during the summer. Digging further down, I found a birthday party celebration at Chuck E. Cheese only a few weeks ago. Looks like the boy had turned eight years old.

There was something about his face that struck some familiarity. I searched but couldn't find any photos of the children's father. Was the father even a part of their lives?

My daughter decided years ago she wanted nothing to do with Keisha's dad. Her father and I were not happy about it, but we supported her. When she got pregnant again, I eventually met the dad. Leesa's relationship with her son's dad was a bit precarious, but I knew they worked at co-parenting these days. So it was strange to me, but not too strange, that there wasn't any existence of a dad on the page. Maybe he just wasn't around.

I looked at the clock on the wall above the television. Then glanced at the door. Amos had been gone awhile now. I wondered how things were going next door. Hopefully, he could get some answers from Briana. She ran out of here like someone had chased her out.

Correction. No, she ran out because Sondra Howell's name had been mentioned. This reminded me why I was nosing around on these people's Facebook pages in the first place. I really wanted to find a connection between Sondra and Briana.

I pulled up my stepdaughter's page. Briana had a beautiful singing voice. She didn't know, but I often went to her Facebook or Instagram page to listen to what she posted. She didn't post every day, but at least once a week Briana shared her soul in a video with strangers. She'd spent so many years in California, hoping to pursue her dreams. I'd heard that Nashville and Atlanta were also major places for musicians and singers to pursue their craft. I knew Briana clashed with Amos when she was younger and took her mother's death hard, but I always wondered why she didn't pursue her career a bit closer to home. I assumed since her older sister had married and moved to Seattle that the West Coast made more sense to Briana.

But was that the only reason?

I scrolled down her Facebook page which was filled with videos she'd posted over the years. Some videos showed her singing on stages with a band while others showed her singing alone, possibly in her L.A. apartment. In recent videos, I recognized the living room in Amos's old home. Briana was sitting on a stool with a guitar in her arms. She strummed the strings effortlessly, singing a song I wasn't familiar with, but it sounded pleasant and soothing to the ears.

This was a talented young woman who most of the time seemed bent on self-destruction. Obviously, life didn't go the way Briana had expected. I knew from her older sister that Briana had money issues since she constantly reached out to her sister for assistance. What still didn't make sense to me was her abrupt move back to the East Coast. No doubt living rent free in her childhood home seemed like a good thing, but Briana needed to grow up some. She may be forced to after last night's discovery.

I'd noticed there were some photos I hadn't seen before on Briana's page. I clicked the post to find a group of photos. In one of the photos Briana was smiling and Theo Nichols had his arm thrown around her neck. They definitely knew each other and seemed quite the couple. In another photo, Briana stood between both Theo and Damion. Glancing at the post, I realized these photos had to be taken this past weekend. This definitely proved both men were at the house.

I wanted to take a closer look at the other photos, but a noise pulled my attention away. I cocked my head, listening to the sound, finally recognizing the front door lock being turned. Amos had returned. By the look on his face when he entered the house, I knew things hadn't gone well next door. I shut the laptop.

Amos plopped down in his chair and turned on the television. "Briana didn't want to talk. She wants to put this all behind her." He rubbed his hand across his bald head. "I told her if she's holding back something, Detective Wilkes would find out. There's nothing I can do if she doesn't talk."

By now I was bursting at the seams. Between my Facebook digging and the statement Amos made earlier in the kitchen, my inquiring mind had to know what was going on. "Amos, what did you mean earlier about not getting her out of trouble *again*? What kind of trouble was Briana in before that could come back to bite her?"

I knew he heard me, but for an awkward minute it seemed like he had no intentions of responding. I'd been around Amos long enough to know it took him a minute to think about what he wanted to say. Still, it irked me to have to wait.

A deep sigh rose up as if the memories pained him. "That Nichols boy was a bad influence on her."

I guessed, "Theo?"

"Yes, there was some kind of party back during Briana's senior year. A girl, someone Briana knew, was killed."

I sucked in a breath, but held my tongue despite the rapid fire questions roaring through my mind.

Amos continued, "Briana and this girl didn't get along. They even fought a few days before the girl's death. Both girls had been suspended. I punished Briana, and she wasn't allowed to leave the house except to go to school. I was on a case that night. It was a Friday and there'd been the usual football game. Briana was supposed to be in her bedroom, but she snuck out to see Theo after the game. You know he was a big time football player back then, a running back. He and Damion entertained people at his house all the time. Anyhow, I got a frantic call from Francine. She didn't know where Briana was, only that she wasn't in her bedroom. I left my partner to hold down the investigation while I searched for her."

Amos rubbed his hands across his bald head. "I had a hunch and I was right. Sure enough, I found her at Theo's house. Unfortunately, something had gone down before I arrived at the Nichols' boys house. That girl Briana had the fight with ... she'd been shot."

My laptop was still in my lap, so I placed it on the couch beside me. Then, I scooted forward practically to the edge of the couch, "Oh no, Amos."

"Briana claimed she was with Theo, and they both were somewhere else in the house." He shook his head. "No telling what they were doing. I didn't want to know. Really, I only wanted Briana to have a tight alibi, which she would have had if she'd stayed home like I told her." Amos's voice rose, the memory of what Briana had done still affected him.

"The girl who had been shot was outside with other kids, just shooting the breeze in front of the house. Witnesses claimed the bullets came flying from nowhere and everyone was ducking for cover. The final findings were the girl was shot by a stray bullet. No one knew or saw anything. All the kids outside were questioned, and somehow Briana's name kept coming up."

"Because of the fight a few days before? People wanted to blame her?"

He nodded, "Yeah. It helped that I was a homicide detective and everyone knew me. Knew us. They'd watched Briana growing up. She'd been a good kid. I don't know what happened to her when she got with Theo. I know girls go crazy over guys, but he changed her. She would have never left the house like that. To this day I don't know what the girls were really fighting about, but one of Briana's teachers at the time seemed to think they were fighting over him."

I cringed, "Fighting over a boy ain't never did any girl or woman any good. So, do you think someone is going to dig this up? I mean Briana wasn't officially charged with anything."

Amos shook his head, "No, there's no record. But people talked a long time, and people around here have long memories. I really think that's why Briana took off after graduation. I wanted her to go to college, but she wanted to explore the world. She came back here when Francine got sick. Took care of her mother, she really did. She's a good girl, now a woman. I don't know what drives her to make the impulsive decisions that she does. She has done damage with that mouth of hers, but I know she wouldn't ... kill anyone."

I felt a lump in my throat. Amos had been fighting doubts about his own child and I hurt for him. "You know your baby girl, Amos." I asked, "What's next?"

Amos stared at the television, but I'm sure he wasn't seeing the screen. "I'm going to have to figure out what's going on. Why was that woman at the house? Where was she really killed? Who had motive? I know how this works, Eugeena. I know if I was Detective Wilkes I would be looking at all the obvious clues."

I gazed at Amos's profile, worried that he had to go through what seemed like a repeat of the past. A past that included Briana's old flame and another dead female.

Chapter 9

Booming music met my ears when Amos drove into the Nichols Brothers Auto Shop parking lot on Wednesday morning. Outside of the shop were slick sports cars of various models that I wouldn't know. A slim young, caramel-colored man splashed a soapy cloth across one bright red car with shiny silver rims. He glanced back as Amos parked his truck in one of the spaces outside the shop. When Amos climbed out the car, I observed him give a head nod to the young man, who grinned and returned one back.

So far, so good.

The male greeting between the two put me slightly at ease. The test would be when Amos ran into Theo. After hearing the story last night of Briana's past dealings with Theo, I was anxious about our visit today. Before heading to bed last night, I did some searching. I felt like I remembered the death of a young girl who had been shot.

Yvette Hunt.

Her face nor her name registered with me. I wasn't the only Social Studies teacher at Northwood Middle, so I assumed I'd never taught her. Unfortunately, Charleston had a high crime rate for as many years as I could remember. It was hard to keep up with every tragedy.

There were similarities surrounding her death and Sondra's. One being the Nichols brothers, mainly Theo. Yvette Hunt had been shot almost ten years ago in front of Theo's house, a guy that she liked enough to get into a fight with another girl. Was it really just a random shooting the way it was filed officially?

While Theo seemed to stay clean, I'd heard about Damion's shady dealings over the years. He'd served some time for minor drug possessions and aggravated assault. He happened to be outside during the shooting. Since it was in front of their house, were the bullets meant for one of the brothers?

Despite Amos's protests, I was determined to join him this morning. Sitting in a waiting room wasn't my idea of fun but I had two valid reasons. One being to keep Amos out of any trouble and two, my curiosity needed to be satisfied. I hadn't been around these two brothers in years. Last time I really saw them up close was their graduation almost a decade ago. I used to make an effort to see former students at their graduations, especially the ones that had difficulty in school. It was a huge milestone.

Theo's high school career was beyond successful and he had attracted all kinds of attention. I'd heard through the grapevine, Theo had the best intentions of making it big with football, but his stint ended after college. Theo bounced back with opening his own business and eventually brought in his younger brother. The brothers seemed to run a successful business.

I followed Amos into the auto shop towards the counter. To my surprise one of the brothers was at the counter. His hair was slightly different, same close cut but the blond streaks were gone. His black t-shirt was rolled up displaying muscles.

Damion looked up as we approached, "Hey folks, what can I do for you today?"

I had to look up since the man towered over the counter. His smile was bright, but there seemed to be wariness in his eyes that didn't match his smile. Either he was tired or this young man had grown accustomed to keeping some distance. I wondered if he recognized me.

Then it occurred to me. This man was hanging out at Briana's a few days ago. He had to know Amos was Briana's dad.

While I observed the man, Amos stated, "I've been interested in getting a paint job for my Chevy Silverado out there. Wonder if I could get an estimate?"

Damion shifted behind the counter like he was onto Amos's ploy. He looked past us out the window. "Sure, we can do that. How's the engine running? Do you need anything else done? Tires?"

"Nope, Old Betsy runs fine out there."

Old Betsy. I sighed. It wasn't until after we were married that I noticed Amos had names for objects. Why he named his truck Betsy, I didn't know. One day I thought I heard him talking to the lawn mower, calling her Lucille. That was his favorite toy of them all. Our lawn always looked good though, so no complaining on my part.

"Is Theo in?" Amos asked.

I bristled next to him. *Really, he was just going to walk in here and ask for Theo?*

Damion frowned, "Not yet." He looked at the clock, "He comes in a bit later in the morning."

Amos peered down at his watch. "You know what, there's a dent on the right side of the truck bed that I've been meaning to get looked at for a while now. Someone bumped into the truck while it was parked at Walmart a few months ago. Maybe you can look at that too. About how long will it take to give me an estimate for both?"

Damion nodded, "Not too long. Why don't you have a seat and I will let you know when Theo arrives?"

As Amos and I walked over to the waiting area I could have sworn I felt the young man's eyes on my back. When I turned around, another customer had arrived drawing his attention away.

I sat next to Amos and whispered, "I think he knows who you are."

"Yeah, I know. Probably doesn't like that I'm a former cop too."

Made sense to me. The waiting room was a pretty nice setup with comfortable seats. Across was a counter filled with bottles of water, a basket of snacks, a coffee pot and condiments. I was eyeing the snacks when a young lady came around the corner holding a broom and dustpan.

She stopped abruptly in front of me as though I'd surprised her. The young woman stared at me, her eyes were accented with thick long black lashes. The lashes were so thick, it took me a moment to really see her eyes which were red around the rims. She wore burgundy tipped locs that were held up high over her head. I assumed she must work here since she wore a black t-shirt with the white lettering, Nichols Brothers Auto Shop.

I started to become unnerved by her stare and responded, "Good morning."

She asked, her voice unsure, "Ms. Patterson?"

"Yes, I'm Ms. Patterson. Do I know you?"

She stepped forward, beaming at me as if I'd just

presented her a winning prize. "I'm Charlene Hunt. You may not remember me, but I was in your class."

It took me a few seconds to place her, but just like that I could picture her as she was at age thirteen. "Charlene, I do remember you. In fact you were friends with..."

That's when it hit me. Her last name was Hunt. The girl who was killed years ago was Yvette Hunt.

Charlene's face scrunched up as if she was about to do an ugly cry. Maybe that's why her eyes appeared red. She'd been crying. Poor thing! Having to work and obviously upset.

She ventured closer to me, her voice much lower. "You heard about Sondra?"

I glanced over at Amos, who had been looking down at his phone. He shot me a look and then peered down at the phone again.

Okay, I guess this was on me.

"Yes, I heard. I talked to her mother yesterday at church. She told me Sondra had been missing. Last time she saw her was Saturday night. She'd left the house to hang out with some friends."

Charlene's eyes grew wide and she gulped, "Yeah, Sondra started working at the Black Diamond. We were just together on Saturday. It's been a long time since we hung out."

"Oh, if I remember, you two were BFFs in middle school."

She cringed, "We hung out, but we kind of grew apart after high school. I mean we stayed in touch, but she did her thing and I did mine."

I wondered if their split had anything to do with Yvette Hunt. There wasn't a smooth or easy way to broach the subject. Sondra was the reason for this woman's angst.

Focusing back on the manner at hand, I exclaimed, "I'm so sorry for your loss. I just can't imagine who would do such a thing to Sondra."

"Yeah, me neither." Charlene answered weakly.

I wanted to press Charlene more about what happened on Saturday, but was interrupted. Damion opened a side door that led out to the waiting room. At some point he'd left from behind the counter. "Hey, Mr. Jones, Theo just arrived in the back. He will check your truck out in a bit and give you an estimate."

Damion turned his attention towards Charlene. He frowned at her. "You finished in the back?"

A slight smile spread across Charlene's somber face. "Hey, Damion, you remember Ms. Patterson from Northwood Middle?"

The young man slowly tore his eyes from Charlene to look at me like he'd just noticed the little old woman who came in with the old dude. He stepped back and placed his hand over his mouth, "Yeah, I remember you." He pointed at me, "South Carolina history. Man, your class was cool!"

"Really?" I don't recall anyone describing me as cool.

"Yeah, I learned a lot in your class. You taught us the book stuff, but you would also pass on interesting tidbits that weren't in the books too. Like I remembered how you talked about Robert Smalls and the role he played in the Civil War. I thought that was cool for a Black man to be seen as a hero back then."

I placed my hand on my chest, hoping I wouldn't burst out crying. "Why I'm touched that you remember that. He was a very special man in South Carolina history. Not everyone enjoys history, but you have to know your past to know where you're going."

"Yes, ma'am." Damion frowned and cocked his head

as if something caught his attention. "Excuse me for a second." He turned suddenly and strolled toward the front store window.

Charlene must have heard whatever had caught Damion's attention. She leaned the broom she'd been holding against the wall and walked up beside him. She squeaked, "Oh no, what's she doing here?"

With that, I was up out of my seat, peeking around to see what was going on. When I saw who it was, panic struck me. "Amos, you may want to see this."

Amos looked up from his phone and peered at me.

I don't know what had his attention on that phone, but I needed him to pay attention. I pointed and mouthed, "Look."

He walked up behind me to observe what I insisted he see.

I whispered loudly, "That's Sondra's mom."

When his eyes widened, I knew he was thinking what I was thinking. He stated, "We better get out there."

I marched outside behind Amos, my eyes glued on Gladys Howell facing off with Theo. The woman was almost a foot shorter than the large man, but she had her finger directed in his face.

"You did this. I know you did. My daughter loved you and had your kids. You mistreated her and them all this time. I told her to stay away from you. You were going to be her downfall. Look what happened! You killed her. I know you did."

Theo backed up, his eyes blazing. "I didn't do anything to Sondra. Don't you be telling people I did. I never laid a hand on her."

Gladys shrieked. "Don't you lie. Don't you dare. I know.

I know you hit her before." Overcome with rage, Gladys stumbled forward.

Amos and I both rushed towards her, he grabbed one arm and I grabbed the other. Despite our effort, she still sank to the ground.

"Gladys, are you alright?" I begged. Her body shook from the fierceness of her anger, her mouth opened, but nothing spilled out. I stared at Amos, "Do we need to call an ambulance?"

"Yes, this isn't good." Amos yelled at Theo, "Call 9-1-1 now!"

Theo's face was a mixture of anger and fear, but he pulled his phone out of his pocket and began dialing. By this time, the auto shop's employees, including Damion and Charlene, were all standing around watching. No one was working, and I noticed a few of them had their phones out. *Why were they filming this?* I don't know why people's first instinct now is to pull out their phones. But I guess it would have been a good thing if Theo turned ugly. Here I was worried about Amos getting laid out by the big man.

Still the last thing Gladys needed was her obvious grief and anger over her daughter's murder going viral. Despite Gladys's impulsiveness, her motherly instincts may be on to something. I just wished she'd thought of her own health before confronting this man.

I regarded Theo who had begun pacing. Damion had walked over to him, appearing to try to calm his brother down. I couldn't hear what was being said, but I was pretty sure the words coming out Theo's mouth were not pleasant ones. An occasional expletive pierced my poor ears.

So, Theo was the father of Sondra's children. I didn't see that spin on the current situation coming. I was reminded last night that there wasn't a single picture of Theo on Sondra's page, not even with the children. Was that on purpose? Was the man not a part of his children's lives at all? Somehow that didn't strike me as right.

The man ran a family business with his brother. Seemed like family should be important to him.

I turned my attention towards Amos, wondering how he was absorbing the revelations. My husband already didn't like the man, now he was glaring at Theo something awful. I wasn't sure if Amos's anger was because of what Gladys accused Theo of doing or because of the young man being back in Briana's life.

It certainly didn't look good. This was all making Briana seem more and more suspicious.

Chapter 10

This was starting to be a bad habit, one I was familiar with from past incidents. There was no doubt that Amos and I were fully invested in finding out who murdered Sondra now. So invested that sleeping had become a losing battle. Since being retired, I rarely had eight hours of sleep anyway.

I tossed and turned most of Wednesday night, barely getting four hours of sleep. My mind was stuck in a loop, trying to process what turned out to be an extremely long day. Gladys had suffered a mild heart attack outside of the auto shop. I had a feeling that she had been ignoring the pains in her body even when I saw her on Monday at church. The tragic loss of her daughter and then the confrontation with Theo had been too much on her grieving body.

Amos and I stayed with her until some relief arrived. Volunteers from Missionary Baptist including members of the Women's Missionary Society, the usher board and Pastor Jones were more than happy to sit with Gladys. She'd been placed under strict orders to rest, but that was hard for a woman who'd just lost her daughter. I was pretty sure Gladys had been administered some serious medication at the hospital. She didn't appear to notice anyone coming in and out of her room. That might have been a good thing. If I'd just faced down a potential murder suspect for my daughter, I would need to be medicated too.

Once we left the hospital, it was already late afternoon. My mission was to find someone to take care of the kids. Sondra had two children who not only suffered from the loss of their mother, but now their main caregiver had been hospitalized. Amazingly, the Brown sisters stepped up. The children knew them from summer camp, and the twins embraced them as if they were their own grandchildren. I was relieved. I wanted to bring the children back to our house, but I still couldn't get past this triangle that had started to form in my head.

Sondra. Theo. Briana.

Amos said he saw Theo at the house Saturday night, and Briana had been acting peculiar, and not just because she'd found a dead body. There were photos of the two of them on her Facebook page. Something was up and it was starting to make me a bit afraid for what could be in store for us.

As I tried to shake myself awake, other worries assaulted me this morning. Somewhere in the early hours of the morning, Amos had left the bed. I'd flipped over to find his side of the bed cold and empty. I had no idea where he was or how long he'd been up. The sun had started to peek through the blinds. I knew I needed to rise myself, but I just couldn't find the energy to lift my body from under the covers.

My phone rang on the nightstand by my bedside.

So much for being lazy. The Lord has a funny way of getting a person in motion.

I have to say I wasn't too surprised to see my daughter's phone number. *Please don't tell me she needs me to watch the kids* was my first thought, but then it hit me. I hadn't reached out to any of my children to tell them what was going on. If Gladys was privy to what happened to her daughter, I was sure my family had found out from the news reports last night.

I grabbed the phone and placed it to my ear, immediately regretting the shrill sound bursting from the ear piece."

"Mama, what's going on? We need to talk. Why didn't you tell me someone was killed next door? Again? Didn't this happen a few years ago to Louise's son? And what happened at Nichols Brothers Auto Shop yesterday? It's all over Facebook."

I sighed, "Good morning to you too, Leesa. I'm sorry, child. Things have been a little crazy." I sat straight up in bed, "But what are you talking about? What's all over Facebook?"

"Crazy is right! Mama, there is a video with you and Amos in it. Well, you show up later in the video. It looks like you are pulling Ms. Gladys off Theo Nichols. Is she actually accusing him of murdering Sondra? How is she doing anyway?"

My daughter's questions were about to have me dizzy. I slid back down in the bed, my body melting into the mattress from exhaustion. A memory from yesterday struck me. I completely forgot about people holding up their camera phones.

"Mama, are you okay? Is Ms. Gladys going to be okay? This is a big mess."

I sighed, "You don't know how big of a mess this is going

to be. I should probably get with you and your brothers if you don't already know."

"Oh I know. Believe me we all know. Mama, how did Sondra's body end up at Amos's house?"

"Leesa, if I knew, the case would be solved. Look, I can talk to you about this later. I need to drag myself out of this bed and check on Gladys this morning."

"Are you working at the summer camp today?"

"Not today. The Brown sisters are keeping Sondra's children and I needed a break. We have some fill-in volunteers handling the camp today."

"Mama, I need to see you soon. After you check on Ms. Gladys, can you meet me at Good Eats for lunch? My treat!"

Leesa never treats me to lunch, so I wasn't about to turn that down. "That sounds like a plan. Now that I think about it, you have been awfully quiet lately. Are the kids doing okay?"

"Yes, Mama. Tyric and Keisha are visiting with Chris's mama this week, I meant to tell you."

That had me jumping out of the bed. "What? Since when?"

Leesa remained quiet for a half a second too long making me anxious. "They've been in Columbia all week. Chris is bringing them back to Charleston on Friday."

"Okay. It was good to see Chris at Junior's Fourth of July barbecue." My oldest son lives in Greenville with his wife and children. I don't see them as much with his schedule. His wife, Judy, had their daughter last year. I've mainly seen my most recent grandchild, Jessica, on Facebook. Every time I saw the twins, they seemed to have grown an inch or two. We decided a few years ago since

Junior traveled this way for Thanksgiving and Christmas, that the Pattersons would visit them for the Fourth of July.

Leesa cleared her throat. "Chris and I are seeing each other more often. You know, for the kid's sake. We will talk more later, Mama."

We would indeed. This was a new development. At least to me.

Chris Black was the father of Leesa's second child and son. My daughter had a peculiar relationship with him. When I first met Chris he appeared to be an intimidating guy, dressed in his police uniform. Since then I'd only seen him in plain clothes and my initial impression of him had improved.

From what I could tell, Chris always made an effort to be in their lives, but sometimes, especially after Tyric's birth, Leesa seemed to want nothing to do with him. Maybe it was her postpartum depression, but it didn't help that she moved with the kids from Columbia where Chris lived. At the time, with her being the mother of two young children, I wanted to keep an eye on her so I liked that she moved near me.

Both of my sons were happily married and I wanted to see the same for Leesa one day, with the right man. The past few times I'd been in Chris's presence, I wondered if he could still be the one.

I pushed my daughter's love life to the back of my mind and got ready to visit the hospital. As I moved around the house, I noticed how quiet it was inside. There wasn't even any barking or snoring from Porgy. By the time I made it downstairs, I determined that Amos and Porgy must be outside. Instead, when I glanced around the backyard, neither male specimen could be found.

Wandering back around to the front of the house, I saw

Amos's truck was gone. That kind of upset me. The man just took off and didn't say a word. Now I was confident he'd taken Porgy along with him. That little booger loved to sit in the front of the truck with his nose up to the window. I wasn't a fan of riding around with the Corgi in my car, but Amos didn't seem to mind, making Porgy all the more endearing to his new housemate.

I soon found the answer to the missing males on my phone. Amos had sent me a text earlier.

I know yesterday was a hard day. I didn't want to wake you. Porgy and I are going for a ride this morning. Will be back soon.

Okay, well a sister had things to do too. I couldn't be waiting around. I fixed a cup of coffee and then perused the refrigerator for something to eat. I struggled with a diabetes type II diagnosis two years ago, but with weight management and changing how I cooked, I'd been able to manage the disease. Still my sugar levels tended to be higher in the morning which was normal. I decided to go with a cup of plain Greek yogurt, something that I'd acquired a taste for as long as I could add fruit.

Blueberries became my choice of fruit today. I ate slowly, still contemplating Amos's text. I checked my sugar levels again and headed to get ready. It wasn't until I climbed inside my car, almost thirty minutes later, that I decided to return his text.

Amos, I'm heading out to the hospital to check on Gladys. Then Leesa wanted to grab some lunch. I will get with you boys later. Don't get into any trouble.

Before I cranked the car up, a text message arrived back.

You stay out of trouble too, Eugeena.

I laughed sharply. This way of communicating with

technology was something else. I was still a bit upset he left the house this morning without saying a word.

We'd have to talk about that later.

Chapter 11

Pastor Jones was praying with Gladys when I peeked inside her hospital room. I held my head down and joined the prayer. I was always amazed how much our young pastor resembled his dad, the great Reverend Tennessee Jones. He sounded like the man who'd remained at the helm of Missionary Baptist for most of my life. It struck me that Gladys left the church because this young man stepped into the role as pastor. He grew up as a preacher's kid, so he got into a few things before the Lord captured his attention. None of us truly escaped those periods of our lives when we wanted to rebel against it all. We all surely had a past.

Pastor Jones had his own way of pastoring the church which was a bit more modern than his predecessor, but he shepherded his flock with just as much passion. I was happy that Gladys returned to the church. None of us at Missionary Baptist were perfect, but we treated each other like family.

Pastor Jones glanced over at me after closing out his prayer. "Sister Eugeena, it's good to see you this morning."

"You too, Pastor Jones. How's our patient?" I stepped further into the room, getting a good look at Gladys. She still appeared in a weakened state, but more conscious than when I left her yesterday.

She smiled faintly, "Good morning, Eugeena. I owe you an apology."

I frowned, "For what?"

Gladys shook her head, "I don't know what came over me yesterday. I saw the video. I can't believe I acted like that."

Pastor Jones patted her hand. "Gladys, you're grieving. Don't beat yourself up."

A tear rolled down her face. "That's no reason to act like a foolish old woman. I shouldn't have done it."

I stepped closer. "You mean you shouldn't have confronted Theo? So, have you changed your mind?"

The pastor looked over at me and frowned. I'd been warned by Pastor Jones in the past about my sleuthing. He didn't approve of citizens getting involved in police investigations. It wasn't like I picked this stuff out for myself to do. Incidents that involved a dead body kept falling into my lap.

Gladys shook her head. "I don't know, Eugeena. Theo hasn't been around lately, but I know he'd been violent with Sondra before."

"He has? Have you mentioned this to the police?"

Gladys nodded, "I did. I told them everything I knew." Tears spilled down her face. "I saw her, Eugeena. The man pulled that sheet back. My girl was gone. I told her that night she should stay home with the kids. They needed her. If she had stayed home that wouldn't have happened to her. They said someone hit her across the head. I just thought, Theo hit her before and ..." her voice trailed off.

Pastor Jones patted Glady's arm, "Sister Howell, let the police deal with this. You need to remain calm, let your body heal. Your grandchildren are going to need you now more than ever."

I nodded, "Pastor is right. Don't you worry. I'm sure the police will talk to Theo."

Pastor Jones cleared his voice, "Well, ladies, I need to visit some other patients. Gladys, if you need anything else please reach out. As soon as you hear from the police, we can start talking about the services. I will ask the members to continue to pray for your strength."

I waited until the pastor left before I asked any more questions. I didn't want him looking at me disapprovingly. I mean the man was young enough to be my son. That just felt weird. I had my own reasons for finding out more about any involvement Theo may have had in Sondra's death. I wanted to find out if Gladys knew about Briana. Of course, I didn't want to ask her directly. I pulled up the chair that the pastor had just vacated. "I'm not going to hold you long. I have one question."

The woman looked exhausted, but she shifted in the bed to direct her attention towards me. "What is it, Eugeena?"

"When we talked at church on Monday you mentioned that Sondra had mood swings and that she wasn't doing too good. One of the reasons why you left her alone. Do you know if she was upset with Theo about something?"

Gladys nodded. "I don't know. Probably. I heard her yelling at him on the phone one night last week. He was supposed to be spending this past weekend with the kids, but he had something else he wanted to do." She frowned as though she was trying to force herself to recall the conversation, "I overheard her say, 'You got another woman now. This is how it is when you get someone new. Nobody and nothing else matters.'"

New woman.

That funny feeling like something was making my stomach sink was returning again. "Do you think she found out about this woman? Have you known Sondra to have words with the women in Theo's life?"

Gladys looked at me, her eyes suddenly alert. "Theo cheated on her the whole time they were together. I knew of one or two confrontations. You think a woman did something to my girl?"

I shook my head. No way was I trying to put that thought in her head, especially because she didn't seem to be aware of Briana just yet. "I don't know. I just want to figure out what happened."

"Yes, I want to know who took my daughter from me. She was my only child, Eugeena. I don't know what I'm going to do. How can I raise her babies without her? I'm so old."

I reached over and patted her arms. "It's going to be alright, Gladys. You have people from the church helping you and we will continue to be there for you. Right now you have to take care of yourself." I pulled my phone out to check the time. It was time for me to meet up with Leesa soon. "I'm so sorry, Gladys. If you need anything, don't hesitate to call me."

I walked down the hall of the hospital, feeling burdensome. With every step, I had to wonder about the person that confronted Sondra that night.

Chapter 12

When I stepped into Good Eats, Leesa caught my attention at a table near the front. To my surprise, she wasn't by herself. My daughter-in-law, Carmen was also sitting at the table. These two together made me nervous. I loved how my daughter took to Carmen like an older sister. They weren't that far apart in age and Carmen had married Leesa's favorite brother. My oldest boy, Junior, treated Leesa a bit like a second dad, where Cedric had always been Leesa's support system when she was on the outs with me. It would upset me anytime we were estranged over our mother-daughter issues, but I took comfort in knowing Cedric always had the magic touch with his little sister.

I pulled out a chair from the table, eyeing both young women. "This looks like an ambush."

Carmen stood and hugged me. "It's not, Mama Eugeena, but we are concerned. Cedric wanted to call you this morning, but he had two deliveries at the hospital. He's really worried. And yes, we saw the video."

I sat down with a huff. "That video. What is wrong with people whipping out their phones over every little thing? That was the last thing Gladys needed yesterday. The woman was distraught."

Leesa's eyes widened. "Do you think Theo did it, Mama?"

"I don't know, but I need a menu. I'm famished. You're still buying my food, right?" I had to check with Leesa sometimes. It wouldn't be the first time she wiggled out of paying for a meal.

Leesa rolled her eyes. "Yes, Mama."

Leesa and Carmen had already ordered. Despite the smells of soul food tempting me, I decided to keep it simple and ordered a large house salad with grilled chicken. I was in need of some protein to energize me.

Once the waiter took my order, Carmen asked, "How's Amos doing? This all happened on his property."

I cleared my throat. "He's worried, especially since Briana found the body."

Leesa tapped her French-manicured fingers on the table. "That's awful. I don't know what I would have done if I found a dead body."

"Seeing that I have some experience, the first thing you experience is shock at what you are seeing."

"Did she know Sondra?" Carmen asked.

"Funny you asked. She acts like she doesn't, but ..." I peered around making sure no one was listening to our conversation. "There's a common thread between the two women."

Leesa and Carmen glanced at each other and then back at me, waiting for me to continue. But the waiter showed up with our food. I almost wished I had ordered something else besides the salad once I saw what the girls had ordered. Leesa was rubbing her hands together over a plate of chicken and waffles, while Carmen had salmon and grits placed in front of her.

I was too distraught to really enjoy a meal right now and those kinds of meals were not for me anymore. I felt like I was eating just to survive. Once we were all served, I prayed over the food and we dug in, devouring our meals in silence.

My impatient child broke our eating in peace by nudging me, "Mama, you were saying?"

I finished chewing, and then took a swig of my unsweetened ice tea. No doubt I was purposely holding off this conversation. I hadn't voiced any of this out loud to anyone, especially to Amos. I took a deep breath. "Well, you know the father of Sondra's kids is Theo Nichols. I found out from Amos that Briana used to date Theo in high school. He's been coming to the house to visit Briana. In fact, he was just there this past weekend."

Both Leesa and Carmen's eyes grew wide.

"What are you saying, Eugeena?" Carmen inquired.

I waved my hand as if I was shushing a small child. "I'm not saying anything. I made a few observations."

Leesa asked, "What does Amos think?"

I picked up my fork, but placed it back down. I was starting to lose my appetite and that wasn't a good thing for me. I loved to eat, and I really was hungry when I arrived. "We haven't talked about yesterday, nor have we talked about Theo Nichols. I will say that we were at the auto shop yesterday to do more than get work on Amos's truck."

Carmen looked at me, "Amos was already suspicious of Theo?"

Leesa piped up, "I can't believe this. They were all in school ahead of me, but I remember them."

I frowned, "That's right. You were in school with that crowd. What do you remember?"

Leesa nodded, "I was a freshman, and they were all seniors." She held up her fingers calling out names with each finger. "The Nichols brothers, Theo and Damion. Sondra. Oh yeah, and Charlene. You know what's funny? I didn't remember Briana until you and Amos hooked up."

I rolled my eyes at that *hooked up* phrase. "I don't know anything about hooking up. Amos and I were both two different people back then. I was still married to your father and Amos was married to Francine. They didn't move into Sugar Creek until after both their daughters were grown."

Leesa shook her head, "Isn't it crazy how small the world can be? Anyhow, I remember Damion more so than Theo, now that I think about it." She giggled, "Don't tell nobody, but I had a big crush on Damion."

Carmen laughed, "Ooh, look at you confessing your teenage crush. Why was Damion so special?"

Leesa held her hands under her chin as if she was about to drift off into dreamland. "I don't know. I mean Theo was on the football team, but he was so popular. All the girls liked him. Damion was kind of popular too, but he was just different. I thought he had more swag than his brother."

I frowned, absorbing this info. "Damion got into a lot more trouble than his older brother too. Although, Theo had his faults too. He sounded like quite the ladies' man back then if he had two girls fighting over him. Do you remember him dating Briana?"

Leesa thought for a moment. "Honestly, I don't remember Briana being with Theo, but then again Theo was with a lot of girls. I wouldn't be surprised."

Carmen commented, "Sounds like Theo should definitely be considered a person of interest. Does anyone know if he was at the house on Sunday? "

"He was definitely at the house." I answered. "But we know on Saturday, Sondra had been hanging out at a place where she'd just started working. Black Diamond?"

Leesa almost choked on her ice tea. After recovering from a coughing fit, she blurted, "I know that place."

I arched an eyebrow, "You do? You've been there?"

Leesa grimaced. "No, Mama. I haven't been to a nightclub in forever. But I know one of the owners. Mac Porter. He's Chris's cousin."

"Really?"

Chris has family in Charleston. That's good to know.

I wasn't going to mention anything about Chris, but this was the second time in the same day that my daughter mentioned him. I'd been curious about the arrangements of Chris's visits since he and Leesa weren't married, but I knew how Leesa hated me being in her business so I kept my curiosities to myself.

I started eating my salad again, letting the munching drown out my thoughts. Food was my greatest comfort, but I still found myself wanting to return back to what Leesa mentioned, "Sondra started working there a few months ago too."

"You think her death has something to do with the club?" Carmen suggested.

Leesa jumped in, "Maybe she saw or heard something she wasn't supposed to?"

I shook my head. "Okay, you two are just as bad as me with all these hypotheses. Even if your suggestions have some truth, the girl was killed next door. We are still trying to figure out who Briana had over at the house. Apparently, she had some guests she didn't know."

"Sounds like she could have had some really shady characters in the house." Carmen reached down in her pocketbook. "Did you and Amos ever consider the alarm system that Cedric suggested?"

"The one with the cameras? Y'all have a camera it feels like in every window."

Carmen laughed and then placed a pamphlet on the table. I peered down to see Simply Safe Security on the front of the pamphlet. I flipped it open to find a smiling multicultural family inside their home.

Carmen's voice soothed, "It feels that way, but we don't have a camera on every window. We have one in the front, the back and on the sides of the house. I really like having the one in the front because when someone rings the doorbell, I can see who is at the door on my phone app. And it works great to see when deliveries have been dropped off at your house while you're at work."

"That sounds like a lot. And these days usually Amos or I are home during the day."

"Yes, but think what you could have caught on camera if you guys had the security system, not just at your house, but on Amos's property as well."

Carmen brought up a good point. My son bragged about his elaborate system, but I'd been living in Sugar Creek for thirty years and never had a need for an alarm system in the house.

"Mama, why is Briana inviting these types of people in Amos's house? I mean how does she know them? She's been living in California all this time. I don't get her at all."

Leesa was asking some pertinent questions, and I wish I had the answers. I commented, "With the Nichols brothers and a few others, I'm assuming she's mainly connecting with classmates from high school."

My daughter rolled her eyes, "Well, they get together too much. I wouldn't want to see some of the people I went to high school with that much. If I'm not mistaken, Briana's class is due for their tenth year anniversary soon. Why not wait until the reunion?"

"Is that right?" Something else came to mind. I'm not sure why I didn't bring it up before. "Leesa, we were talking about girls that Theo dated. There was a girl who was a part of this same class that was killed. I believe her and Sondra were friends. Do you remember?"

Leesa waved her hands around in excitement, "I do remember. Charlene Hunt's sister. Yvonne, no Yvette was her name. They were twins, but they weren't identical."

I nodded, "So they were fraternal twins? What do you remember about Yvette?"

"She was a cheerleader like Sondra. I don't know why I didn't remember her earlier. Yvette was a real pretty girl. She wore her hair short and had darker skin than her sister Charlene. I want to say she was taller than her twin too. There was some random shooting. I remember for about a week it was so sad at school. A lot of people were crying in the hallway and in class. No one ever found out who shot at the house. Why are you asking, Mama?"

I didn't want to get more into the weeds right now. I'd already shared too much. "No, reason. I saw Charlene yesterday and remembered her being best friends with Sondra."

Leesa frowned. "This is all coming back to me, Mama. Sondra, Yvette and Charlene. Sondra and Yvette were both cheerleaders." Then she added, "They were also known as mean girls."

That sparked my interest, "Really?"

Leesa cocked her head. "Yeah, you know what? Now I remember they used to pick on this one girl all the time. Yvette and that girl finally got into a fight."

I leaned forward, "Leesa, that girl was Briana."

My daughter stared at me. "What? Briana. Wow, I guess I did see her in school, but I didn't really know her name. Mama, why are you bringing up all this old history? What does Yvette's death years ago have to do with Sondra?" Leesa sucked in a breath, "Mama, you don't believe Briana did anything?"

I shook my head, "I don't know what I believe at the moment. I just know there is no such thing as a coincidence."

Carmen had been listening intently with her arms folded on the table. "No, Ms. Eugeena. I don't believe there is a coincidence here. I hate to say this, but Amos should get Briana a lawyer if he hasn't already. If these women were mean girls as Leesa said, there could be some bitter memories for Briana. Either she's guilty of getting some kind of revenge or someone is still messing with Briana all these years later."

I exclaimed, "That's exactly what I'm thinking. Good to know that you both are seeing what I'm seeing. I'm really worried, it doesn't look good for Briana."

If my daughter could remember conflicts from almost ten years ago with some prodding, it's like Amos said, other people probably had long memories too. Suspicion around Briana would only get worse. Thinking back on the list of people who were at the house, I wondered who else could have had a grievance against Sondra that ultimately led to her death.

For Briana's sake, one of her classmates needed to rise to the top of the list.

Chapter 13

Even though I had ordered a salad, my stomach felt full from finally demolishing the rest of it before I left the restaurant. Leesa insisted I finish it or take it home since she was paying for the meal. I had to laugh because I knew that was something she learned from me. I did not believe in wasting food or money.

On the way home, my energy dipped low again, either from the summer heat, the meal or the week's events. Probably a combination of all of the above. There was a time when I used to only take naps on Sunday afternoons. A good nap after Sunday service and a good meal, now that was heavenly. But with my retiree schedule, I took a nap anytime of the week. I needed some downtime right now, but when I rolled into my driveway I could see a nap would not be coming my way anytime soon. Amos's truck was in the yard. Now that he was home, we had to have several conversations, starting with where he went this morning.

Before I could get out of the car, I heard someone calling my name. I turned around to find my neighbor, Louise Hopkins, waving at me from her porch. Sitting next to her was her granddaughter, Jocelyn Miller. Louise had been through some things the past few years including the death of her son and being placed in a nursing home. When her long lost granddaughter came along, Louise's life took a change for the better, gaining a whole new family and her beloved home back. Before I became head of neighborhood watch, Louise held the role. Despite being seventy-two years of age, she still kept a sharp eye on things.

I kind of was surprised Louise hadn't ambushed me yet about the activities earlier in the week. I knew it had to be the aches in her body keeping her more still than usual. She was adamant about staying in the home she'd almost lost and had no intentions of returning to a nursing home. I didn't blame her. I missed my friend dearly and knew she was good where she was, here in Sugar Creek.

I walked up on the wraparound porch steps and reached down to hug the woman I'd known as long as I lived in Sugar Creek. Her blue eyes sparkled at me. "It's good to see you, Eugeena. Come on, sit a while so we can catch up. I've been meaning to come check on you, but the arthritis has been something else the past few days."

I sat down in one of the white rocking chairs Louise had on her porch. Her porch had bamboo ceiling fans that swirled slow and easy, making the hanging ferns sway. I helped myself to some of the lemonade Louise had sitting on a table between the rocking chairs. This woman was a true southern belle, always ready to be hospitable to guests. I guzzled the cold lemonade, "Mmm, this is good." I pointed to the glass, grateful for the cool liquid. "I didn't realize I was thirsty." I placed the glass on the table and turned my attention to the two ladies who were waiting patiently for me to share. "I'm sorry I haven't been by, I know you must have questions."

Jocelyn must have arrived home from her job shortly before I arrived. She sat on the other side of her grandmother still dressed in her uniform, a caramel blouse emblazoned with the Sugar Creek Cafe logo and her brown pants. She peered over at me, "We know you have your hands full. Me and Grams have been talking." Jocelyn rubbed her hands together as if they were cold.

I raised an eyebrow. "Sounds like you two should share first."

Jocelyn grimaced, "This has to be a sensitive time for you."

"Sensitive?"

Louise whispered, "Amos's daughter. We heard she found the body."

I was wondering how many other people knew Briana found the body. "Yes, she did."

Louise scrunched her nose, "The parties, Eugeena. We've had college kids renting houses in this neighborhood for years and they get loud from time to time. Now Briana seems like a good woman, but does she need to have all those people over every weekend? And on a Sunday this past time."

"Believe me, Amos has talked to her. It's a precarious situation with her coming back home after all these years to live around her one remaining parent, the one she's been at odds with the past few years. He doesn't want to rock the boat and have her leave. To be honest, I think she does a lot of what she does to get under Amos's skin."

"She's definitely being difficult." Jocelyn stated.

Usually Jocelyn was in a bouncier mood. She could have been tired from work or even exhausted from the heat, but I had a feeling she had more to say after that statement. "How's Briana doing at the cafe, Jocelyn?"

Jocelyn tilted her head down as if to prepare herself. She shifted her attention towards me, her eyes appeared sorrowful as if what she was about to say pained her. "Eugeena, I'm not sure things are working out for Briana at the cafe."

"Oh no." I had begged Jocelyn to help Briana get a job at the Sugar Creek Cafe. The girl needed something to do. Jocelyn came through a month ago with a part-time position for Briana. At first Briana seemed to want to refuse, but Amos encouraged her to take the job. Plus, I knew the cafe hosted singers and musicians for music night on occasion. It was a perfect opportunity for Briana to acclimate herself to the community.

"She's not been on time the past few days she's been scheduled. She called in sick yesterday, which I understood after what happened Sunday night." Jocelyn peered around me down the street as if she was expecting to see Briana. "There's more. She begged me not to tell her dad, but after what went down Sunday night I feel like I needed to at least tell you."

My shoulder wilted, "I see, so I can be the one to break it to my husband."

Jocelyn appeared sheepish. "Better you than me. You may know how to softly explain to him that his daughter attracts trouble."

I think Amos already knew that, but I surely didn't want to lay anything else on him right now. I leaned back in the porch chair, letting the chair slowly rock my weary body. "What did she do?"

Jocelyn swallowed and looked at her grandmother. Louise gave a slight nod of encouragement. "There was an altercation at the cafe last Monday between Briana and a customer."

I sat straight up, tiredness in my body forgotten. "An altercation. Like a fight?"

Jocelyn leaned forward, "It was almost a cat fight, Eugeena. Coffee was thrown and a carafe broken."

I suddenly wasn't feeling so good anymore. That nap was calling me again. This time, it was more about wanting to hide under the covers. "Jocelyn, I'm too old for this. Just tell me what happened. My brain is already preparing me, excuse my bad grammar, that this ain't gonna be good."

Jocelyn shook her head. "I've been scared about what to do or say. The woman Briana was arguing with was—"

I held my hand up. "Let me guess. Sondra Howell." I finished for her.

Louise sucked in a sharp breath, "How did you know she would say that, Eugeena?"

"Let's just say that my eyes have been opened. Briana's obviously been holding back some information. Y'all, I'm just scared for Amos."

Louise reached over and patted my hand. "I'm so sorry, Eugeena. You two don't deserve this. You haven't even been married six months yet. You both should be enjoying this time of your life."

Yes, that's exactly what I've been thinking.

I took in a deep breath to calm my nerves. "What were they arguing about?"

Jocelyn cringed. "From what I could tell, Sondra was not happy that Briana was back in town. She told her she needed to go back wherever she came from. No one wanted her around here."

"I have to ask. Who threw what?"

"I will say Sondra was the only one that threw coffee. Well, not really." Jocelyn stood and demonstrated. "She smacked the cup of coffee on the counter towards Briana.

In trying to get out of the way, Briana bumped into another employee who was trying to pour an order." Jocelyn shook her head, "That's when the carafe was broken, and the shouting match started."

"I ended up threatening to call the cops. Sondra and the woman she was with left and Briana was pretty shaken up. At first she had an attitude, and rightly so, she'd been threatened at work. But later when she was in the office, Ms. Eugeena, she was crying and that's when she begged me not to tell her dad."

But she needed too. This was information Briana hadn't shared with anyone. If our next door neighbor knew, then someone else probably knew about this altercation too.

What was Briana thinking?

Now it was really time to get to business. I had too much information to just sit still anymore. And I couldn't be worried about being sensitive, even if it hurt my marriage.

Briana had publicly fought with a young woman that she found dead less than a week later in Amos's backyard.

Chapter 14

When I arrived home I found Amos in the kitchen cleaning fish. This man loved frying fish. The fishing poles I saw leaning against the backdoor took care of my questions about where he took off to this morning. I'm not sure why I felt led to keep up with Amos's whereabouts. I tried to do this during my first marriage and at some point I gave up. I was married to an obstetrician whose second home was the Charleston Memorial Hospital. Maybe because I knew that's usually where I could find Ralph if I really needed him, I didn't concern myself with his coming and goings.

Amos was so different from Ralph. For one, we literally had been partners-in-solving crimes prior to getting married. This new development of a body next door was indeed complicated, but I figured we'd solve this thing together. Instead, I could feel something loosening the seams of our marriage, creating a chasm that wasn't there a few days before. I didn't like it. I could've blamed it on the old insecurities that cropped up in my first marriage, which was quite distant for a number of years. But I knew that I needed to be concerned.

I spotted Porgy in the corner admiring his male cohort at work. These two were the best of buddies.

"I take it y'all had a good time fishing today."

Amos turned and grinned, "Yeah, I needed to think."

I should have known. It didn't even occur to me earlier to search for the fishing poles which remained outside in the shed.

I placed the Simply Safe Security pamphlet Carmen had given me on the table. I had so much I wanted to say, but I needed to start somewhere and I didn't want to put my foot in my mouth, which I was frequently guilty of doing.

While he washed his hands, Amos glanced over at the pamphlet. "I've seen that before. Cedric gave me one."

"Yeah, well I have been highly encouraged to consider getting a security system now. Carmen brought up a good point today about the cameras. Think what we could have captured the other night."

Amos grabbed a kitchen towel from the drawer by the sink and began drying his hands. "A camera would have come in handy Sunday night for sure. Not sure what good it would do now."

Before I could pour out my conversation that I had with Jocelyn, Amos shared some news. "By the way, I got a call from my buddy on the force. They just picked up Theo Nichols for questioning."

I arched an eyebrow. "Okay, I guess Gladys got Detective Wilkes' attention."

"Yeah, but Theo is denying he had any contact with Sondra last weekend. He was over at Briana's most of the weekend and claims Sondra never entered the property. In fact, he said the last time he saw Sondra was for his son's birthday party."

I pulled out a chair from the kitchen table and sat down.

I tried to recall the photos I'd viewed on Facebook a few days earlier. To my recollection, I didn't recall seeing one photo of Theo. "I saw photos at Chuck E. Cheese on Sondra's Facebook page. There wasn't a single photo of Theo."

"That doesn't mean he wasn't there."

I tipped my head to the side, "So, you don't think he's lying?"

"About not seeing Sondra this weekend? I'm not buying it. How else would the woman have ended up in the shed? She had to arrive at the house on Saturday night, the last time she was seen alive. Who had motive?" Amos threw the kitchen towel back on the hook and sat across from me at the table. "This is my theory. I think Sondra came to confront Theo. Maybe she showed up outside and they went out in the backyard where no one could overhear them arguing. The argument grew heated and he pushed her down. Hard, making her hit her head. I still haven't figured out where or what she hit her head on. The more I think about it, she could have been struck on the head with an object."

I grimaced, "So someone walked away with a murder weapon?"

He shrugged, "Probably. They had to hide it, so their fingerprints and/or DNA couldn't be found."

I nodded, "Makes sense." I shook my shoulders, "I guess I don't want to believe a father would do that to his children's mother. I know, I know. It happens all the time especially in domestic violence cases. I guess I'm stuck on the young man I watched grow up who had been a high school football star. When we were at the auto shop, he looked like he was doing well as a businessman."

"I'm not saying he intentionally tried to hurt Sondra.

Maybe he was angry that she showed up while he was trying to get back with Briana. I don't know, he could have panicked and in his haste to hide her body, pulled her inside the shed."

"I don't know, Amos. If he supposedly likes Briana, why would he leave Sondra's body for her to find?"

"Maybe he didn't want her to find the body."

I peered at him, "What?"

"Briana mentioned everyone just decided at once to head out, some had jobs the next day. Suppose someone placed Sondra in the shed with intentions of returning the next night when the coast was clear."

I nodded, anxious to know where he was going with this theory. "So, the killer was going to come back and bury her someplace else?"

"Right, but they weren't expecting Briana to go outside. She said she hadn't been in the yard since Friday."

"Okay, but—"

"But what, Eugeena?"

Lord, help me. That was all the prayer I could muster, because I was too tired right now to have this conversation, but it could no longer be avoided.

"I've had several conversations today. I know Briana is your baby girl, but she's not been completely honest with the police or you. Amos, I feel like you need to get her a lawyer. ASAP."

He frowned, "What's going on? Briana didn't have anything to do with *that* girl's death. I know my child. She may be a bit high strung, but she wouldn't hurt anyone."

I placed my hand over his hands, which were balled into fists. "I don't doubt Briana's innocence, but she's not been honest with Detective Wilkes, and it's going to come back to bite her. First of all, it is clear that Briana knew exactly who Sondra was when she saw her body. They went to high school together. Sondra was Yvette's friend. After yesterday's incident with Gladys, you know Theo is the father of Sondra's two children. Gladys told me she overheard Sondra being upset about some new woman in Theo's life. Who has Theo been coming to see on a regular basis, Amos?"

Amos closed his eyes, "I admit that Briana should have been more upfront."

"You think? When Detective Wilkes asked her if she knew the woman, Briana was purposely vague. I saw the detective's face, and you and I both know how tenacious that little detective can be." I took in a deep breath, "That's not all. Just now, Jocelyn—"

"Jocelyn? I thought things were working out fine at the coffeehouse."

I shook my head. "Amos, Briana and Sondra had a very public altercation at Sugar Creek Cafe last Monday. Jocelyn has not said a word because Briana begged her to remain quiet. But you know at some point in this investigation Detective Wilkes is going to find out. I know you think Theo should be going down for this, but Briana needs to come clean because I have a feeling..."

Amos's face turned stony. It caused me to pause for a moment. I knew he wouldn't have an outburst in anger, but a shutdown was on the horizon. His eyes glazed over as if he couldn't take another word I was telling him. But I had to finish my statement for me.

I gulped, "Detective Wilkes is going to be looking at Briana as the number one suspect. She found the body. Don't you detectives always suspect that person first? I know a few years ago, Detective Wilkes sure was looking at me sideways after I found Mary in her house. You know

Mary and I hadn't spoken to each other in years. I looked guilty."

We sat in silence for some time, until it started to feel uncomfortable. Even Porgy looked sorrowful at us from the corner. I knew Amos was seething with anger, either at me for bringing this to his attention or at his daughter for not being honest. I suspected both.

I stood from the kitchen table unsure of how deep the gash was I'd just placed in my marriage. But I had to tell him everything I knew, I wasn't into keeping secrets.

"I'm going upstairs to rest for a while. I'm sorry about all of this. Maybe deep down Briana's just scared, Amos. Remembering what you told me about the past, maybe she wanted to come back to Charleston in peace. The only thing is, since she's been back, she's ran into and in some cases clashed with people she left behind almost ten years ago. I'm going to pray for her. We're all going to need prayer."

I trudged upstairs, my heart feeling heavy. Behind me I heard the patter of paws on the steps. The one thing about Porgy, he could sense a person's mood. He knew when I was upset. The little dog took advantage of the occasion to climb up on the bed. I was too tired to yell at him to get off. After undressing, I climbed into bed despite it being late afternoon.

I didn't know how long I'd been asleep, but when I awoke my eyes focused on the reddish tones in the sky as the sun made its descent for the evening. I needed to close the blinds, but was too lazy to move. I stretched my feet and noticed Porgy was still on the bed, but so was someone else.

"Amos?"

Why was he sitting in the dark?

I fumbled for the lamp switch on my nightstand. The bright light caused my bleary eyes to water.

Amos turned around, "Sorry, I didn't mean to wake you."

I rubbed my eyes and stifled a yawn. "I needed to get up anyway. What's wrong? Did you talk to Briana?"

"Yeah, I went to talk to Briana."

I sat up. Something about Amos's tone alarmed me. His voice was tight with tension and a hint of something else. Fear? "How did it go? What did she say?"

Amos turned full around to face me. "She's gone."

Alarm bells clang inside my head. "What do you mean she's gone?"

He shook his head, "She took Francine's car. I looked around the house, and it looked like she may have packed a bag."

"Oh no, Amos. Why would she do that?"

Amos sighed so deep I felt it. "Probably because of this." He passed his phone to me.

I reached for it and peered down at the screen. There was screeching. But it wasn't from inside my head; it emanated from the phone. I studied the figures in the video and recognized the teal blue and brown décor, *Sugar Creek Cafe*. There on the screen was Briana behind the counter. Her eyes were wide. Across the counter, a woman stood shouting. I could only see her side profile, but I was fairly certain this was Sondra.

I snapped my head up, "Someone recorded the argument last Monday."

"Yeah, and Wilkes has the video."

"How did she get it?"

"Someone sent it to her anonymously."

I stared as I watched what Jocelyn had described to me

play out. An angry Sondra slapped a coffee cup on the counter sending what had to be hot liquid flying. Some of the liquid seemed to hit Briana despite her scrambling to move out of the way. Sure enough, glass crashing could be heard next. I could barely hear what they were saying, but one thing I heard over and over from Sondra, almost like a chant, "You should have never come back here."

I paused the video, staring at the screen some more. "Amos, I don't have your kind of experience, but this feels like a setup. Who recorded this video and sent it to Wilkes? We have to find Briana. Where would she go?"

Amos rubbed his head. "I have no idea. I'm going to go back to the house to see if I can dig up any clues."

"That's a good idea." I snapped my fingers, "Where's the list you got from Briana?"

Amos reached into his pocket and unfolded the list. "Why?"

I reached for the list noticing the paper appeared frayed around the folds like Amos had been opening and closing the piece of paper often. Since I last saw the list he'd placed an asterisk by Theo's name.

"Theo is getting the heat right now probably because of Gladys's accusations. How long will that last?"

Amos frowned, "Not long. Wilkes is focused on Theo, but I'm afraid things are about to shift to Briana. I just don't understand why she took off."

I didn't understand why Briana took off either. She'd only made things worse and made herself appear even more guilty.

Or was she guilty?

I couldn't think like that. If Amos believed in his daughter's innocence, then so would I. I examined the list as if I expected one of the names to jump out at me. There was someone on this list that had to be the guilty party. Whoever he or she was, they were doing a good job of shifting blame to Briana.

My eyes focused on one name in particular, and I determined that I would seek this person out first thing tomorrow.

Chapter 15

Briana stayed gone all Thursday. Amos called his eldest daughter, Alexa, but Briana was not responding to her sister's calls either. For some reason, I felt like Briana would return. When I checked the house, I noticed more of her things were still around including her guitar. It didn't strike me that Briana would leave anywhere without her prized guitar.

That brought some comfort to Amos when I pointed this out to him. I'd never seen his stress levels like they were now. I believe if he wasn't already bald, he would have rubbed his hair clear of his head.

My theory was Briana needed to get away and gather her thoughts together. She didn't get along with her dad, but that's because she was just like him in a lot of ways. Though I doubted Briana had gone fishing.

While Amos spent most of the day searching in places he thought she might have gone, I decided to follow-up on my hunch from last night.

But before I could begin my little inquiry there was something else I had to do. When I talked to Gladys at the church on Monday she mentioned Sondra hadn't kept in touch with friends, and she blamed it on Theo. Now that I knew the tragic circumstances of Sondra losing her best friend in high school, I was curious to know more about the breakdown in friendship between Sondra and Charlene. Especially since Charlene openly admitted her and Sondra had been out of touch.

Was it because of Theo? Or did the loss of Yvette break up the friendship between the two young women? I still couldn't recall ever seeing Yvette in school, but I had brief flashes of Charlene being with Sondra. Sondra was what I would call the dominant friend, while Charlene seemed to be more like a puppy, satisfied with following the leader. Where Sondra had a mouth on her that could inflict damage, I rarely heard Charlene speak, but I recalled her egging Sondra on in support.

What really puzzled me was how Sondra became involved with her childhood best friend's love interest. How did that make Charlene feel to see Sondra grow close to a young man that her sister Yvette loved? Sure, loss can bring people closer, but something about that relationship seemed off. It was obvious there was animosity between Sondra and Theo. I felt sorry for the poor kids. I could only hope that the two co-parented in some type of peace.

That video from the coffee shop was also bothering me. Sondra fiercely confronted Briana in the coffee shop a week ago. Why? These were two adult women with almost ten years between them of never crossing paths. Was the altercation about Theo or was there still lingering blame for the loss of a childhood friend? Amos said people were suspicious that Briana had something to do with Yvette's death.

Now that Briana had returned, it almost felt like someone was getting back at her. Sure, I didn't know her like Amos, but I had my doubts the child would knock someone in the head only to call her father over to see the body.

I really didn't want to burden Gladys with all the questions swirling around in my head, especially since the woman was grieving and recovering from a heart attack. But as Sondra's mother, she had to be aware of the dynamic between Sondra, Yvette and Charlene.

Did she really suspect Theo had something to do with Sondra's death? It wasn't really clear why, and when I talked to her a few days ago, even Gladys wasn't sure why she went off on the man.

When I walked into the hospital room, Pastor Jones was by Glady's side. I was glad to see him offering support to a woman who a few years ago had left his flock for really petty reasons.

They both turned to find me in the doorway. Whatever smile I may have had on my face slowly started to fade. My gut churned with dread, especially when I noticed the concern on Pastor Jones' face. Had Gladys's health gone downhill since I last saw her?

Whatever way the woman was feeling, the fiery stare Gladys sent me spoke volumes. I recognized this Gladys from years ago. She'd always been a hell raiser, and her daughter inherited her mouthiness from her mother.

I tentatively stepped into the room, "Good morning, Gladys."

Gladys continued to glare at me, slowly shaking her head as if she couldn't believe I was standing in front of her. I glanced at Pastor Jones who looked from me to Gladys like he wasn't sure whether to run or stand between us.

"Gladys, remember what your doctor said," he soothed.

"I remember," she snapped. "I also remember telling this

woman I needed help finding my daughter who she already knew was dead."

My heart dropped clear down to my stomach. When I talked to Amos about this, something in the back of my mind told me I should have said something to Gladys. "Now wait a minute, I didn't realize that it was Sondra ..."

"She was your student. How could you not remember her? I know. You wanted to make sure you protected *that* murderer."

Gladys was a grieving mother and if I were in her shoes I would want justice too. That means going after the person who appeared the most guilty. I stepped back, "I'm not protecting anyone. I really didn't know it was Sondra. She looked ... familiar to me." I couldn't tell this woman how I found her daughter, with those vacant eyes and the horrible gash on her head. "I encouraged you to tell the police. I know the detective on the case and I know how diligently she works to solve her cases. Besides, you stood out there the other day and accused Theo Nichols of doing Sondra harm. He was there at the house too."

Gladys shook her head vehemently, "He's not the only one. *That woman*, what's her name, Briana, she probably worked with him. They worked together to get rid of Sondra."

I shook my head, "No, I don't believe that's what happened." I frowned, "What would be their reason?"

Gladys wailed, "They wanted her out of the way. That's why Sondra is dead. My stubborn daughter kept going after that man. She had two of his kids and he still didn't want her. But I couldn't tell her anything. She wouldn't listen to me."

I closed my eyes, shaken by Gladys's anger and grief.

"I'm so sorry about Sondra. The police will discover the true story."

She sat up in bed, shaking her finger at me. "The story is you all are covering up something. You are just trying to protect your new husband's daughter," she spat out.

I shook my head. "We want to know the truth as much as you do. Someone took your daughter's life. I intend to find that person."

"Get out. We know who did it. Theo and *that woman* did it. Trying to pretend they're innocent."

By this time Gladys's anguish had made enough of a commotion that I watched as a nurse hurried into the room straight towards the vitals equipment. The full-figured nurse stared Pastor Jones and I both down, speaking firmly, "I think you both need to leave. Mrs. Howell is too distraught to have visitors at the moment. We can't have her getting this upset. It's not good for her heart."

Pastor Jones, who'd been standing helplessly by, urged me out of the room. I was too embarrassed to say anything to him so I found myself walking down the hall next to my pastor feeling like some scolded child. It wasn't until we entered the elevator that Pastor Jones spoke, "Ms. Eugeena, Gladys is grieving. She didn't mean some of what she said."

I nodded, "I know. She has a right to be upset, but she doesn't have all the facts. The police don't even have all the facts."

Pastor Jones said, "No, but they will."

Because I didn't have a chance to ask, "What made her this upset? Did she see the video?"

"The one from Sugar Creek Cafe?" He nodded, "Yes, she called me this morning. I was planning to visit her this afternoon, but she needed to talk to someone. Someone sent her the video."

I frowned, "Someone sent it to her? How?"

Pastor Jones sighed. "Apparently by text. That's pretty evil, upsetting a grieving mother like that. That was not how she needed to see her daughter."

"No, she didn't." Someone was purposely trying to lay the groundwork to build a case against Briana. No better ally in their corner than the mother of the slain woman.

We walked through the lobby out of the hospital. I had a moment where I thought about touching base with my son, Cedric, who was an obstetrician at this same hospital where his father worked before he transitioned. His wife, Carmen, worked here as well. Let's just say I was in need of some family at the moment.

I was still shook by Gladys's anger, knowing deep down I deserved it. But I really meant her no harm. Something occurred to me once outside in the hot sun. I held one hand over my face until I could dig my wraparound sunglasses out of my bag. Once my eyes were protected from the blazing sun, I asked, "Pastor, could Gladys tell who sent the text?"

Pastor Jones shook his head. "Funny you asked that. I asked her that same question because I couldn't fathom why someone would do that. She said she didn't recognize the number."

The sun was beating down, and I should have been moving with a swiftness towards my vehicle where air condition awaited, but it was like my feet were glued to the sidewalk. I was grateful for my large goofy wraparound shades because I was close to a watershed moment. It wasn't like me to get emotional. I wiped sweat from my forehead and then from the side of my face. I was fairly certain there were some tears mixed in with the sweat.

Pastor Jones must have noticed my approaching meltdown moment, he encouraged, "I know this is all upsetting, Ms. Eugeena. Give all your burdens over to God and he will care for you. He will comfort Gladys. It will take some time for healing to begin. The truth will come out. In the meantime, I pray for peace for you and Amos." He smiled, "You two are still newlyweds. This has to be a shock for both of you."

My pastor had no idea. Really up until now, Amos and I had no major arguments or fights between us. I was here to support him, but I could tell this was taking a toll on us.

"Thank you, Pastor. We appreciate your support."

I watched as my pastor walked away before I started towards my car. It wasn't that far, but I felt baked, from the heat and my encounter with Gladys. I blasted the air conditioner on high and practically pressed my face against the vent. Once I felt my body temperature cooling, I sent a text to Amos.

I'm leaving the hospital. Gladys was really upset. She saw the video too. I hope you are able to find Briana soon. Keep in touch!

I waited.

No reply.

I was too upset to drive away from the hospital, so I called the person I knew could help reign in my emotions. Cora was technically my aunt, but being two years older than me, she was more like a sister. She picked up on the second ring, "Hey, Eugeena, we've been waiting for you to call us."

By we, I knew Cora was talking about her and my other living aunt, Esther. Esther was the oldest living relative I had and was taken care of by her younger sister. "I'm sorry I haven't been over in a few weeks."

"Don't worry, we know you have been enjoying being a newlywed."

I smirked, "Well, I was enjoying it."

"Oh no, I was afraid something was going on, especially when I talked to Leesa last night."

Leesa often got along better with Cora than me. "I'm not surprised Leesa talked to you."

"Yeah, she told me some of the things about Briana and this guy named Theo."

"That's why I'm calling. This is getting out of hand. I just got blasted by the victim's mom, Gladys Howell. Cora, I had this feeling in my gut when I talked to Gladys on Monday, but how can you tell somebody you suspect the dead body found next door could be their daughter?"

"Sister, that's a tough call. Nobody wants to be the bearer of bad news. I imagine it was better for her to hear that officially from the police."

"That's what Amos said too."

"Well, don't beat yourself up. The woman lost her daughter. Wasn't she her only child too?"

"Yes, and she really has it out for Briana who hasn't been the most honest person in the world. Still, I don't believe that child hurt anyone."

Cora agreed, "I only met Briana a few times and she seemed quiet, but you could tell she had some resentment towards Amos. Sounds like she's had a hard life and misses her mom. Why do you think she's not being honest?"

"I believe the girl is carrying around a world of hurt and some mistrust. From what I gathered, this girl found in the shed was one of the same girls who bullied her in high school. In fact, it was a group, a trio of girls. One of them died before they all graduated. Briana got some blowback from the girl's death since the girls had been fighting a few days before."

"What? Wow, Eugeena, that's a lot."

"Yeah. Briana and I didn't hit it off that well when we first met last Christmas, but I've been trying to make her feel at home. I have to admit sometimes she just annoys me because she doesn't try on her end. But I feel for her now. I do want to help her."

"I know you do, Eugeena. Believe it or not she knows this too, even if she doesn't show it. Just pray for her. You know how you had trouble with Leesa all those years ago. You two are closer than ever now. Briana just needs someone to be in her corner too. Sister, ain't no better person to have in their corner than you. Does she even know that you are going out of your way to find the truth?"

I smirked, "And how do you know this?"

Cora laughed, "Eugeena, you ain't fooling nobody. I've known you all your life. I also know since you found Mary a few years ago and hooked up with Amos, you got a thing for solving crime. Almost like you missed your calling."

"First of all, where do you get off saying I hooked up with Amos? That's Leesa's line."

"Well, you are married to the man now. You being the person who thought she'd never get married again."

I had to laugh at that myself. "I'm so glad I called you. I wasn't doing too good and life is even more complicated now."

"Oh! What else is going on?" Cora asked.

"You can't tell a soul."

"Who am I going to tell? Okay, well, Esther is going to

want to know all about this when she gets up from her nap. She's been cross at not hearing from her niece."

I sighed, "Okay, just keep this between you two. We need all the prayers we can get because Briana left."

"Left? Left the house? The city? Not the state?"

"Girl, I don't know. Amos is trying to find her. I hope he can find her soon or the girl is going to look like she's running away."

"Oh my! This is worse than I could have ever imagined, Eugeena. Why did the child run away? She's a grown woman. Better for her to stand and prove she's innocent."

"I think those past issues, on top of Sondra showing back up in her life, are probably making her run. I have a hunch about something that I need to investigate."

"Investigate? Now what are you up to, Eugeena. You are not nosing around in places you don't need to be. Does Amos know about this hunch?"

"Not yet. Besides, I told you he's worried about his daughter and that's all he needs to be concerned about right now.

"Be careful, Eugeena. You aren't even an official private detective."

"No, but I'm definitely going to get some answers."

"Well, be sure you are taking care of yourself, Eugeena. You check your sugar."

Always the nurse, despite being retired herself. "Thanks, I will do that and grab some food to eat."

"Alright now, stay hydrated, Ms. P.I."

I laughed and placed my phone on the car seat while I rummaged around in my bag. I wasn't stopping anywhere for lunch, but I kept supplies on hand. Digging into a bag of almonds, I munched and drank some water feeling a lot more settled in my spirit. That's what I needed. To talk to someone. We all need to have that someone.

I checked my phone again. Amos still hadn't responded to my text, and just like that I started to feel my spirits slipping again. Now I understood why Leesa complained when people didn't return her texts. Although her complaints centered around the fact she didn't get an instant response, I wasn't concerned about Amos getting back to me quickly. But I was bothered that he hadn't replied by now.

I knew his mission today was to find Briana, but I hadn't been privy to what Amos had been doing the past few days. Not that I was trying to keep tabs on the man. That wasn't my thing at all. Still, I was curious why I'd seen him glued to his phone.

Oh well! I still wanted to do something productive today, and this morning had been a complete bust. While there wasn't anything wrong with my Camry, I was about to take a visit to a certain auto shop.

I needed to dive more into these so-called friends of Sondra and Briana.

Chapter 16

When I pulled into the Nichols Brothers Auto Shop, it seemed vacant compared to the bustling atmosphere from only two days ago. I wasn't sure if I should exit my vehicle or not until I caught movement inside. It appeared someone was probably looking back at me, wondering what I was doing in the parking lot.

I didn't leave them long to figure out. I climbed out of the car, once again questioning why I was running around in this hot weather. The humidity had my t-shirt stuck to my back by the time I approached the door.

I frowned at the closed sign. It was a weekday and I knew they were supposed to be open since there was also another sign indicating their operating hours from 9 am to 6 pm. It was past the lunch hour by now, but the auto shop didn't strike me as the type of business to close down. I pulled on the door anyway.

Locked.

I peered inside and then jumped back.

Damion Nichols was looking back at me, his face a mixture of hostility and confusion.

I smiled and waved at him, hoping he would take pity on an old woman.

He relented and unlocked the door. "Can I help you, Ms. Patterson?"

"Are you open today?"

He glanced around the parking lot as if he was expecting a car load of people to arrive and break down the door. "Why don't you come in out of the heat?"

I was grateful. Damion might have had a bad rep, but somewhere along the way, he still remembered his manners.

"How's your brother doing?" Now I didn't mean to ask that, but that's how my mouth worked. Words came flying out before I could stop them.

He eyed me. "Why are you asking?"

"I'm concerned. Briana is my stepdaughter, you know, and she's having a hard time with all of this. I understand her and Theo were getting close since she's been back in Charleston."

Damion sighed, "Yeah, they been hanging out. He's doing as fine as he can, I guess. His lawyer is working to get him out of there. They can't hold him much longer. He didn't do anything to Sondra and they don't have evidence. Plus, he doesn't even know how she ended up at Briana's house."

"Well, that's good. You know Briana found Sondra. She also had no idea she was there at the house and from what I saw on a video, those two shouldn't have crossed paths anyway. I mean why would Sondra show up at Briana's house?"

Damion shrugged, "Who knows. Sondra was crazy."

"Crazy?'

He walked back behind the counter as though he needed to put distance between himself and me.

"Theo and Sondra have not been a couple for a long

time. They were on and off. Really, if Sondra never got pregnant with the kids, I doubt Theo would have had anything to do with her. I warned him to leave her alone. She would always do dumb stuff like not let him see his own kids and then claim he was a deadbeat dad. He takes care of his kids and makes sure Sondra gets a hefty check every month. I'm not trying to speak ill of the dead, but Sondra talked a lot of smack that wasn't true at all. Then her Mama would come right behind her acting like Theo was the worst man ever. Even she wouldn't allow him in the house to see his own kids."

Wow, I wasn't expecting all that.

"Sounds like Theo is getting a bad rap."

"Yeah, hopefully the cops will let him go soon." He looked at me. "I hope Briana doesn't get harassed by the cops. Sondra was known for starting stuff. Whatever went down, I'm sure it wasn't Briana's fault."

"No, it wasn't. Which brings me to another question."

"You're not here at all to get work on your car, are you?" Damion smiled, but I noticed unease in his eyes.

I was not Ms. Popular with folks today.

"Like I said, I'm concerned, and to be honest, I'm looking for Charlene."

Damion's shoulders jerked, "Why?"

I gave him the eye myself, wondering what that reaction was about. "She seemed upset the other day, like she wanted to talk. Sounds like her friendship with Sondra hit a bad patch."

He narrowed his eyes, "Charlene will be fine. She hadn't been that close to Sondra for years. Like Theo, she was better without her."

"I thought I remembered Sondra and Charlene hanging out together when they were younger. But I don't remember Charlene's sister, Yvette. I didn't realize Charlene had a twin until my daughter mentioned it."

Damion scoffed. "Sondra and Yvette, now those girls were two of a kind, they lived for causing trouble for other people. Charlene was and still is sweet. She followed behind those two like some puppy dog. Really, she's better off without both of them."

"Even her own sister? That's pretty harsh to say, Damion."

He shrugged, "Sorry, I tend to say what's on my mind. Yvette's death was tragic, but there were a lot of people who didn't miss her. A lot of people aren't going to miss Sondra either."

I was speechless. Damion was hard core.

"You sound protective of Charlene. She's special to you."

He smiled, this time his face appeared to be genuine. "Charlene and I have always taken care of each other. Like I told you, she'll be fine after some time passes by. She spent years not having anything to do with Sondra."

"So why get with her this past weekend after so much time had gone by?"

He shook his head. "I don't know."

"Would it be possible for me to talk to her?"

He licked his lips, thinking. "I can't tell you where she lives or anything like that."

"No, I wouldn't expect you to do that. But if you can pass the message along that I would like to talk to her, that would be wonderful. I do really want to make sure she's alright. I like looking in on my former students from time to time. I'm glad to see you're doing good, young man."

He flashed that charming smile again. "I'm doing alright."

"Good, well I'm going to leave you and thank you for having a talk with me." I turned to leave.

"Ms. Patterson?"

"Yes."

"Briana's a good person. Always has been. I hope the cops leave her alone."

"You know her dad is a former cop. I'm sure he's going to do all he can."

Damion nodded.

I could feel his eyes on my back as I left the auto shop. Once inside the car, I glanced up. He still seemed to be sitting behind the counter. I still didn't get why the auto shop was closed. Now that I think about it, the whole time Damion and I talked there wasn't a sign of any employees or any noise from the garage. Absolute silence.

I wasn't sure what to make of the shut-down. Maybe Theo wanted everything shut down until he could finish with the police. He was the main owner. It certainly would keep anyone from asking questions and being nosy during business hours.

That didn't stop this old lady.

I checked my phone and smiled. Well, at least Amos finally returned my text. He must have texted me while I was talking to Damion.

I opened the locked screen to read the text.

Eugeena, no signs of Briana yet. Please keep an eye out for her if she comes back to the house. I'm working on something with my buddies and may be late. I didn't want you to worry if I didn't arrive home by dinner.

I stared at the small screen for a few moments. *What was Amos doing that he wasn't going to be home for dinner?* The man was retired.

Lord, wherever he may be please protect him. Protect Briana, and please let me keep my peace of mind.

Chapter 17

Now I should have headed home but decided at the last minute to stop by Sugar Creek Cafe. I occasionally treated myself to a sugar free iced coffee. As hot as it was today, plus my emotional roller coaster ride through the day, I deserved a treat.

The door chimes sang to me when I stepped in. The melodic vibration was always welcoming. Sugar Creek Cafe was not trendy and sleek like the popular franchise coffeehouses. Instead, it was like walking into someone's home. There were various tables, all round, some small and others wide. Each table was fitted with high-back wooden chairs that reminded me of the chairs from my grandmother's house. Along the walls of the coffeehouse were booths with high backs for privacy. If you really wanted to make yourself at home, in the back of the coffeehouse were sitting areas that included couches and plush seats.

There were people scattered around the cafe, most armed with a phone in their hand, some with laptops and others appeared to be having real conversations with their coffee companions.

The person who came up with the decor and started

the coffeehouse was as eclectic as the interior. Fay Everett happened to be a student of mine, probably one of my oldest students. She was in my eighth grade class when I was still a very young teacher. Fay loved the bohemian look and over the years had grown locs that fell down near her waist. Today, she had them tied above her head. She'd always worn glasses and was one of those people who liked to make a fashion statement with her frames.

Both Fay and Jocelyn were behind the counter. Fay blinked at me, her eyes wide and bright behind turquoise, cat-eye shaped frames. She grinned like a Cheshire cat, "Hey, Ms. Patterson. It's so good to see you today. You are looking good. Retirement *and* marriage seem to suit you just fine."

"Thank you, Fay. Good to see you too. I see the cafe is continuing to do well."

"It sure is. Always busy in here. Now I know you like iced coffee. Sugar-free, right?"

I smiled, "Now, that's why I will always give you my business. Girl, you have a memory on you!"

"I don't know about that. I'm pretty sure I remember because you were and always will be my favorite teacher."

"Oh, you don't know how much that made my day." While Fay went off to make my iced coffee, I turned to Jocelyn who seemed more upbeat today. I asked, "Glad you're still enjoying working under Fay?"

Jocelyn stepped forward, "I love working here, and I owe you for sending me towards this place. You know I've had some jobs that I can't say I'm proud of."

When I first met Jocelyn a year or so ago, she'd been working at Hooters. She had a few years of being lost, and I was happy she'd come around and started to see the cafe as more of a step up in her career. I pointed to her, "Being promoted to manager is a pretty big thing, you should be proud."

"I am." Her smile disappeared as she approached me from behind the counter. She lowered her voice so no one could hear but me. "Have you heard from Briana today?"

Oh boy! "No, was she supposed to be working today?"

Jocelyn let out an exasperated sigh. "Yeah, that's what Fay and I were talking about before you arrived. Briana's on the schedule. I hate to do this to her because she's going through a rough time, and I definitely know about that. Been there and done that. Still, this position needs to be filled by someone who's going to show up."

My heart sank. I kind of knew this was coming when Jocelyn talked to me about this the other day. I couldn't tell her Briana had run off. I wanted to give Amos time to find her and not alarm other people that she could be a person-of-interest or even a suspect. That reminded me of another reason why I decided to stop by the cafe.

"Do what you need to do, Jocelyn. Amos and I appreciate you helping her out. Hopefully when the dust settles around her, she can focus on her future."

Jocelyn stared at me, "Is she going to be okay? I saw the video has made rounds."

"You saw it too? Where did you see it?"

Jocelyn glanced back. Fay seemed to still be working on my iced coffee. She pulled out her phone. When she showed me her phone display, I recognized the Facebook interface. "Fay and I were talking about this earlier today too. Right now, no one has approached us about the video. We think nobody knows this happened here, but at some point someone is going to say something."

I nodded, "The cafe has a unique interior. I'm sure someone will say something. I noticed a lot of people are on their phones in here. I guess anyone that day could have recorded the argument. Did you notice anyone who may have been recording the fight between Briana and Sondra last Monday?"

"No. I had my attention on Sondra, who was acting like she was about to tear up this cafe."

"You told me the other day she had a friend with her."

"Sondra's friend? Yeah, she was shorter than Sondra, rather thin and she didn't really say anything. She was wearing false eyelashes. They were pretty long, and you almost couldn't see her eyes."

That had to be Charlene!

"Where was she at when Sondra was hurling insults at Briana?"

Jocelyn thought for a moment. "I remember her getting her coffee first; she must have gone to get a table. In fact, it wasn't until the carafe was dropped that she appeared. I remember her trying to pull Sondra away like she was afraid, but Sondra kept snatching her arm back. By then I was threatening to call the police. That seemed to stop the squabble."

I had a pretty good idea that it was Charlene who was with Sondra, which made me curious again about their friendship. I was under the impression the night at the Black Diamond was the first time they'd gotten together to hang out, but they were here together at Sugar Creek Cafe a week before.

Did they come here to grab a coffee beverage or did they step inside on a mission?

Before I could focus my thoughts more, Fay placed my iced coffee on the counter. "Here you go, Ms. Patterson. Sorry it took me awhile. We have a new girl today and she needed help with the register."

"Oh, I could have helped her." Jocelyn quipped. "Sorry, I started talking to Ms. Eugeena. We were talking about..." Jocelyn dropped her voice again, "the video."

Fay rolled her eyes. "That video. You know I'm all for publicity for Sugar Creek Cafe, but that's not the kind I want. Never in the ten years I've had this place open have I had that kind of drama. It's a shame. I feel bad for Briana. She's been doing good, but I think that incident has shaken her up. I can tell her confidence is gone."

I nodded, "Those women also bullied Briana when she was younger."

"What?" both Fay and Jocelyn responded.

"Yeah, a lot of bad memories. Hopefully we can get Briana back on track. "

Fay smiled, "I'm all for giving people chances. We need the help, but I'm not shutting her out yet. When you see her, tell her to check in with us. We do care about her. And that girl can sing. I've been trying to get her to do a mini-concert here one weekend."

"She does have a beautiful voice. How much do I owe you?"

Fay smiled, "It's on the house today."

"Thank you. I appreciate you treating an old lady. Ladies, I'm not going to hold you up. I'm going to sit a bit and get out of your hair."

I moved past a woman who had her table covered with papers and was tapping away on a laptop. Another table I passed, two women were chatting back and forth and giggling about something.

One of my past times was people watching. As I shimmied into a chair in the back, I wished I'd been people watching a few days ago when Sondra walked in. Since it was the thing to do, I pulled out my phone and soon found the video in question. I watched the video on mute. I mainly wanted to see the video from the angle in the coffee shop. I almost jumped up from my seat when I realized whoever recorded the video had to be sitting in the same sitting area where I was currently. But who? And how were they able to send the video to the police and Sondra's mother? Did they intentionally upload this video to social media for all to see?

The cafe wasn't chilly, just enough coolness to be comfortable. Still, I shivered as if a blast of cold air crawled down my shirt. I'd even looked around me to see if a vent was nearby. There wasn't that I could see, but I knew the real reason why I'd been chilled.

Someone was really setting Briana up in the most awful way possible. Why?

I had a sneaky suspicion I knew who was behind the video recording, but what didn't fit with my growing theory was why Sondra lost her life this past weekend.

Chapter 18

It was a quiet evening.

My husband was missing-in-action like his daughter. I had no clue where he was or the reason behind his cryptic text earlier. I loved that he was considerate enough to warn me that he would be late, but I needed details too. Like where did he think Briana had gone? And, I gathered from his text that his being late had something to do with another matter entirely. In fact, Amos has been preoccupied for a few days prior to his daughter's disappearing act. He was either looking at something or talking to someone on his phone.

Another mystery!

I think one mystery at a time was enough for me. This one was turning out to be the most frustrating because I knew all the people involved, and most of them were my former students.

I fed the dog and made a peanut butter sandwich. My children always teased me about not including the jelly. I'd always just wanted the peanut butter since I was a little girl. It was one of those nights. I didn't see a need to cook. I guess I'd been spoiled since my wedding night. Amos had always been here for dinner. So much had happened today that I wanted to share. With all his detective experience, he knew how to read people.

Doing my best to remain positive, I tried to enjoy my time alone. I intended to spend it snooping and started digging on my most favorite place online. Determined not to be sucked in by anything else on the feed, I returned to Sondra's Facebook page, which was filled with people expressing condolences for the young woman's untimely death.

I scrolled for some time before something caught my eye.

Charlene Hunt.

She'd left a message. I wondered if Sondra's long time, on and off friend would share her grievances publicly.

She did.

Sondra, I'm sorry. I can't believe you're gone. Now I really feel alone.

I read the post again. Why was Charlene sorry? Was she sorry her friend was killed or was she apologizing for something else? I was a bit alarmed by her feeling alone. Had this young woman been grieving her twin sister all these years even though she'd been gone a decade? Sondra was the closest person Charlene would have had in her life who was also close to Yvette.

I clicked Charlene's name, landing on her profile page. What struck me first was a public photo that had been posted about three weeks ago. It was a photo of Charlene, Sondra and Yvette. Sondra and Yvette were dressed in cheerleader uniforms, while Charlene was dressed in jeans. It was a curious photo because Sondra had her arm slung around Yvette while Charlene stood to the side, smiling awkwardly. It was almost like she didn't belong, but had been included as a part of the photo anyway.

I noticed she'd tagged Sondra, but when I looked at the comments I didn't see where Sondra had responded. Maybe she didn't see it.

I know people tag me on posts and after a while I just get annoyed with the notifications.

Further down her page, Charlene had posted pictures of her with her twin when they were little girls. Though they were fraternal twins, both girls were still dressed alike in typical twin fashion. I read Charlene's post.

It's been ten years since you've been gone. Never forgotten, Sis.

I scrolled to see if I recognized names in the comments. My head was starting to hurt from all this digging. I'm not sure why, but I never saw Sondra's name. I got the impression that Sondra didn't interact with Charlene on Facebook. Though I recalled Charlene and Sondra being close during middle school, the friendship appeared stronger between Sondra and Yvette in high school.

My memory wasn't what it used to be. I could be remembering the girls wrong.

Maybe as they got older Sondra no longer had anything in common with Charlene. Cheerleading would be an activity that kept Yvette and Sondra closer.

Despite my growing exhaustion from the day, two names popped out as I continued to scroll through comments.

Both Theo and Damion had responded to Charlene's post about her sister.

Theo: Your sister was so much fun. Still miss her.

Damion: I know you're hurting. Hang in there. Love ya.

I had to smile at Damion's response. Based on the conversation I had with Damion earlier, who clearly didn't like Sondra, I could tell he was very fond of Charlene.

I closed the laptop, ready to head to bed. I had suspicions about Charlene earlier, mainly because I felt like she could have recorded the fight at Sugar Creek Cafe.

So what if she did?

She may have been using the recording to protect her friend if Briana had retaliated.

But Briana didn't. Sondra initiated the argument.

Sondra also ended up dead.

I was beyond confused and exhausted. As I brushed my teeth, my thoughts went to Briana and her past history with these women. There had to be some lingering animosity towards Briana over Yvette Hunt's fate years ago even though it was a random shooting. I wanted to be convinced it was all related and recent events shouted setup to me. Other thoughts lingered though.

Could Briana have tried to defend herself against a raving Sondra and it all went wrong? Why else the secrecy and running away?

I kneeled beside the bed after getting dressed for the night.

Lord, protect Briana wherever she may be hiding out. Only you know her heart. Give her peace in her spirit and comfort in knowing that you will be there to guide us. Lord, I don't know where Amos is, but I know you know. I pray you wrap your arms around him and protect him too. I can't go to bed with any animosity in my heart. Forgive me, Lord. I'm casting all my cares on you. In Jesus Name, Amen.

Amos snuck in after ten o'clock. I knew this because I heard him creep into the bedroom. I'm not sure what startled me out of my sleep. Maybe the sound of his clothes hitting the floor or the fact that he turned the light on in the bathroom. My eyes were immediately drawn to the clock by the side of my bed. I wanted to jump out of the bed and ask him what was going on, but I didn't have the energy.

As sleep snatched my consciousness again, I thought Briana got this thing about keeping secrets from her daddy too.

Chapter 19

When I awoke, Amos had already arose, making me wonder if the man even slept. It was Friday and my previous certainties of Briana's return were waning. Maybe she did really leave and not taking her guitar was symbolic of something else. In fact, the more I thought about it, Briana seemed to have given up on pursuing a career. She still shared her voice with the world, but it was much more scaled back now. I prayed the events from these past two weeks had not stripped Briana of the one true thing where she found joy.

On my way out of the bedroom something caught my eye out the window. I peered down to see a Simply Safe Security van in our driveway.

Did Amos call them anyway? Why didn't he say something?

Okay, I was ready to get some answers. If that van was here, then Amos was somewhere on the premises.

Sure enough, when I arrived downstairs Amos was talking to a representative dressed in a blue uniform with the Simply Safe Security badge on his shirt. I decided not to interrupt and moved on to the kitchen. I needed some coffee.

To my surprise Amos had started the coffee already. I

knew he was perfectly fine with starting the coffee, but it seemed to be something I always did. Grateful for the ready-made coffee, I grabbed a cup and slurped with my ear cocked towards the conversation down the hall. Sounded like Amos was discussing cameras.

A few minutes later, he showed up in the kitchen.

"Good morning," I commented, giving him the eye.

With a sheepish look on his face, he replied, "Morning. You look like you have questions."

I raised my eyebrows. "You think? Don't get me wrong, I'm happy you decided to get the security system, but I'm puzzled by the change of mind."

He sighed, "Have you had breakfast yet?"

"No, I'm about to get something. Why are you changing the subject? Amos Jones, I know you're keeping something from me. I don't like it! We can't be keeping secrets."

He held up his hands. "Woah! I'm not changing the subject. I promise I'm not trying to keep secrets." He wrinkled his eyebrow, then grabbed my hand. "This past week has thrown me for a loop. I do have something to tell you but we need breakfast first."

I rolled my eyes at him before responding, "Now you're trying to scare me. Let me get something started."

A few minutes later, I'd stirred up an old favorite, cheese grits. When I needed some comfort food, it usually involved cheese. Nothing like something that sticks to the tummy to make it all better. Well, at least temporarily.

I prayed while I nuked the turkey bacon. Prayed for peace of mind. Amos was right about this past week. Life had been almost too peaceful since our wedding this past February. I had plenty of years and experience to know worry didn't solve a thing. The one ailment I didn't have and had no plans of ever having was an ulcer.

Nope. Not me. Keeping up with my sugar levels was enough health conditions for me.

Despite my determination to remain calm and let God have his way with me, I still almost jumped out of my skin when the toast popped-up from the toaster.

Ugh!

All the while I moved around the kitchen trying to busy myself with breakfast, Amos sat with his phone in his hand. I peered over his shoulder as I placed his plate of food in front of him.

I asked, "So, we have a camera on the front of the house?"

"Yes, one in the front and the back. And I had two installed on the outside of the house next door too."

I tried to eat my food, but anxiety was making it hard to finish. I placed my fork on the plate with a bang, which I didn't intend to do. "Okay, I can't take this anymore. What's going on?"

Amos peered at me and with a sigh, he pushed his almost empty plate away from him.

Glad one of us had an appetite!

"First, don't be alarmed. But I did look into if there was anyone I put away that could be out for me."

I raised an eyebrow, panic already rising. "And?"

"Nothing has come up yet, but you were right about being proactive. A young woman lost her life right next door. It could have been Briana. Anyways, the boys and I have tried to dig up what we could without Detective Wilkes having a major fit. But, I did come across some info."

"Someone who could be the killer?"

He shrugged, "It came across my mind, especially when I saw the timing. There is a guy who was recently paroled.

He missed showing up to meet his parole officer on Monday. Joe and I have been staking out his last known residences and locations."

I should have known Amos was up to something with his old partner. Despite retirement, it was hard to completely step away from the profession. Amos wasn't about to turn down an investigation, but why was he pursuing this when his daughter needed him?

I frowned, "Shouldn't the police be doing that? If he's messed up his parole, then they should be trying to get him back in jail."

"That's the problem. They don't know where he is."

I twisted my hands. "Who was this guy? What did he do that made you decide to get Simply Security out here today?"

"J.C. White."

I paused for a moment as my memory kicked into gear. "J.C.? Wait, I knew a fellow that went by J.C. Is his full name Jermaine Campbell White?"

"That's him. You know everybody. Was he a student of yours too?"

"Yes. I remember him. He was a bit of a class clown. Same class as Theo."

Amos nodded. "They paroled him on good behavior. He'd been sentenced about eight years ago for drug possession."

"Okay, why are you focusing on him?" Then I sucked in a breath. "Do you think he had anything to do with Sondra's death?"

Amos nodded, "They had to have known each other from school. J.C. didn't graduate but was in the same class with Theo, Sondra, and Briana. When I heard J.C. had been missing since Saturday, I wanted to see if he was tied to Sondra."

I nodded. "Interesting. You think he went missing about the same time Sondra was killed?"

"Not only that, he was last seen at the Black Diamond that night."

"Black Diamond? Same place Sondra was at on Saturday. There's really no such thing as coincidence. I see why you've been preoccupied. You always seem to be looking on your phone. I guess this explains why."

He smiled, "Reading reports, looking at leads. That Black Diamond one seemed like a big lead for me." His smile faded, "But J.C. seems to be in the wind. Last night proved to be a complete waste of time. We were hoping to spot him. Joe thinks the guy has fled the state. My priority is to find Briana and keep her safe. Something is going on with this group of classmates of hers. I don't know what, but I've not seen this level of trouble surround a group in a while."

I nodded, "It is very strange, especially with this class approaching their tenth high school reunion. Sometimes it takes a small group of toxic people to stir the pot, make it worse for the entire group. I know Briana has to be feeling some kind of way returning back home to all of this. No idea about where she's gone at all?"

"Well, I know she hasn't left the state. I had one lead yesterday although I don't like it. She was seen talking to Theo Nichols yesterday, who has been officially moved off Wilkes' list."

My eyes grew wide, "No. Why?"

He shrugged. "I know, and I'm not sure why. He is the last person she should be contacting."

I sighed, "I didn't tell you about my day yesterday.

When I was at the hospital, Gladys practically accused both Theo and Briana of being in cahoots in Sondra's death. As though they wanted to get rid of her."

"I don't like Theo, but I wouldn't put this on him to purposely get rid of the mother of his children. Now if they got into an argument of some kind, I can see an accident."

I agreed, "That does make more sense. When I talked to Damion yesterday, he helped me gain some perspective. There is more than one side between Theo and Sondra. In fact, after talking to Sondra's mom and then talking to Theo's brother, I came up with very opposite reactions. Definitely a case of blood is thicker than water."

I noticed Amos's eyes had grown wide. "You talked to Damion without me?"

That's all that man heard.

"I wasn't planning on talking to him. I went by the auto shop to find Charlene and Damion was there alone. The shop seemed to be closed for the day. I thought that was strange."

Amos fumed, "I don't like this. I can't believe you went over there alone. I don't care for Theo's involvement with Briana, but I have to admit he's a decent guy. A ladies' man, but he's also a shrewd businessman and has deep roots to his community. Now his brother, Damion is just bad news."

I rolled my eyes. "I know Damion has done some time. People do change. If you want my opinion as a former teacher, I believe Damion's way of escaping the shadow of his older brother resulted in him being the exact opposite."

Amos eyed me. "I agree they are definitely exact

opposites. Even if you were his teacher, you didn't need to go by yourself."

"Well, Amos, unbeknownst to me, you went traipsing off with Joe to do your investigation." I pointed my finger at him. "You know me by now. I had to do my own digging. Besides, it was the middle of the day and he seemed amiable to having a conversation. I definitely know that he didn't like Sondra. He didn't have one good thing to say about her. On the flipside, he was complimentary about Briana."

Amos grunted. "You said you were looking for a girl named Charlene. Is this the girl that was at the auto shop the other day when we were there?"

"Yes. If you can recall, she mentioned hanging out with Sondra Saturday night. I want to reach out and talk to her. I figured since she was a former student of mine maybe she would be willing to talk. She certainly seemed to want to that day in the shop. If I can reach out to her, maybe we can find out who was around Sondra that night. You said we needed to trace Sondra's steps from when she was at the Black Diamond. Where did she go Saturday night if she didn't go home? Have you been able to find out anything?"

"I'm afraid J.C. had me preoccupied the past few days."

"I could be wrong, but when you told me about the events from Briana's past and what's happening now it just seems like this ties together somehow. Charlene is the sister of Yvette, the girl killed that night. I've been nosing around. Charlene didn't have the best relationship with Sondra either. I remember Sondra being abrasive. She just rubbed people, sometimes even teachers including me, the wrong way."

"I agree it would be good to nail down what happened

that night. Charlene doesn't appear to be on Wilkes' radar though."

"I wonder why because here's where it gets really weird. Jocelyn said that Sondra left the cafe with a woman. From the description, that woman had to be Charlene. I believe Charlene recorded the fight, but I don't see why she would share it unless this is her way of getting back at Briana. You said people were blaming Briana for Yvette's death."

Amos frowned, "Yeah, I can say that's suspicious of Charlene recording the fight. Maybe she did it to protect Sondra if things got ugly." He looked at me, "What are you thinking? Are you seeing Charlene for doing something? Why would she kill her own friend though?"

I shook my head, "I have no idea. This is your area, reading people. I find it peculiar that Sondra and Charlene hadn't been in each other's lives until recently. What changed? Could Yvette's death have driven a wedge into their friendship? Remember Yvette and Briana were fighting over Theo. Yvette's dead. Briana moves on. Who ends up with Theo? Sondra. After talking with Damion, Sondra didn't exactly win over Theo. She had this really weak connection to Theo only through their kids."

Amos rubbed his hands across his head. "That's too much drama to process. This is what I solidly know. Sondra's death strikes me as someone reacting in a fit of passion, probably real anger. I haven't given up on Theo being angry enough to shove Sondra down. Sounds to me like Damion only supported the theory that Theo had enough hostility built up to hurt Sondra."

"I admit Theo does seem like the more likely subject. But there's no evidence. Do they know if Sondra was struck with an object?"

"More like she fell on something. She was probably shoved hard."

"So it could be a male or female?"

"That's right. Her clothes will not be processed until a few weeks. It's possible forensics could pick up something from the other person having contact with Sondra."

We sat in silence for a few minutes, letting everything we talked about settle in.

I finally broke our quiet moment of reflection. "You said there's a few weeks on the forensics and they let Theo go for now. How long is it going to be before they start to bother Briana again?"

Amos heaved a sigh. "Not long." He turned his phone in my direction. "We have company."

I turned my attention to the camera display on his phone. "Oh boy." Sure enough Detective Wilkes was standing outside her car looking directly at our house.

Chapter 20

Lord, Jesus help us. Please don't let it get ugly in here!

I prayed my desperate pleas as I followed Amos to the door. We already knew Detective Wilkes had to be here looking for Briana. What would Amos say?

We stood by the door, barely breathing in anticipation of the detective ringing the doorbell. We had enough drama going on but the last thing we needed was to try to push this woman away. With our track record, Wilkes might want to throw both of us in jail.

Even though I was expecting her, looking over Amos's shoulder as the detective approached our front door, I still practically leaped out of my skin again when the doorbell rang. I stepped back, watching as Amos opened the door.

"Good morning, Detective. Can I help you?"

Detective Wilkes peered in through the screen door, her eyes scanning behind us as if she knew we were hiding something. Or rather someone. "Can I come in, Mr. ...er, Detective Jones?"

I arched my eyebrow. Amos had been retired from the force for five years. Knowing she wanted him far away from her case, the acknowledgement of his former title was highly suspicious.

"Why, sure. Come in, Detective Wilkes." Amos opened the screen door, allowing the diminutive woman passage into the house.

Wilkes continued to let her eyes roam as she stepped further into the house. I met this woman about two years ago and she hadn't changed a bit. She kept her red hair tied in a ponytail. The only thing different was the woman had given up on her blazer. We were in the middle of July, and even the calm, cool detective had the sleeves of her white shirt rolled up to her elbows. I noticed a slight shine on her face. It was indeed a hot one out there.

Amos stretched his arms towards the living room chairs. "Why don't you have a seat? I'm assuming you have some updates."

My husband was one cool cucumber, having a conversation with Wilkes as though there wasn't anything wrong. I followed suit and sat down on the couch next to him as Wilkes seated herself in one of the chairs across from the couch. I decided I would do something I didn't normally do. I would keep my mouth closed. This was Amos's daughter's life on the line and I didn't want to mess up anything.

"Thank you for inviting me in. Unfortunately, I can't share too much about the ongoing case. I know you know by now the identity of the young woman."

Amos nodded.

Wilkes smiled, "Of course, knowing you and my dad, I'm sure you are aware of a lot more than you're letting on."

I didn't see a problem with Amos hanging out with his old partner, Joe, but ever since I found out Lenny Wilkes, a former detective himself, was Detective Wilkes' dad, I'd been a bit sketchy about the man. I hoped Amos hadn't been talking too much to Lenny. It didn't seem like a good idea if the man shared anything he knew with his daughter.

Amos grinned, "You know Lenny and I meet up on occasion to share war stories."

"Mmmm, yeah, I've heard about those war stories. My dad is also not shy about asking me questions about cases, which brings me to the reason why I'm here."

Uh oh!

Silence settled over the living room after her statement. Amos and I waited. I wanted to fidget, but I matched Amos's calm demeanor as best I could. It was like Detective Wilkes wanted to create the most impact by taking her time to state her reasons. I don't know why; all three of us knew she could only be here because she was looking for Briana.

She cleared her throat. "Jones, I've been trying to get in touch with your daughter, Briana. Any ideas where she may be?"

Amos cocked his head as though he was thinking. "Unfortunately, my daughter is a grown woman. I can't say I keep up with her whereabouts."

Wilkes' facial features changed as if she was disappointed in his answer.

I don't know why! Nobody was going to give up their child to the police.

"It's really important that I speak to her. We have had some developments in the case."

"Yes, I've heard. And I've seen the video, Wilkes."

I was surprised by Amos's directness.

"I'm sure you have as well as a lot of other people." Wilkes shook her head. "Your daughter didn't reveal to us that she knew the victim. We need to question her again now that we know she had an altercation with the victim."

Amos responded, his voice a bit gruff. "There was no altercation. I saw the victim slinging hateful words at my daughter in a place of business."

Wilkes shot back, "That had to be humiliating for Briana. From what I dug up, there's a history with Sondra Howell. In fact, I believe it goes back to high school. Look, I realize Briana was bullied by Sondra and some of her peers. That has a lasting effect on a person. My theory is Briana had enough, especially when the victim entered her property last Saturday."

I couldn't hold my tongue. "How do you know if they had contact with each other that night?"

Wilkes turned to me as if she just remembered I was in the room. "Ah, Eugeena! Well, I don't have to tell you your stepdaughter had a party or get-together at her house. I've been in touch with your neighbors and this went on each night this past weekend. A few people who were in attendance mentioned that Sondra was at the residence on Saturday night."

This was news to me. I mean I knew Sandra had to have walked on the premises at some point.

Amos inquired, "So you have witnesses who said Sondra was on the property, but you don't seem to have witnesses that stated they saw the two women together?"

Wilkes snapped, "Of course the women saw each other. How could Briana not see who was at her house? From our count, there were at least fifteen people at the house on Sunday night. That group wasn't so large that your daughter couldn't have seen Sondra at some point during the night. That's why we need to talk to her. Something went horribly wrong. If anyone was in her shoes, the last person you'd want at your house is a known enemy."

Amos stood. "I'm sorry, Wilkes, I respect you, but you don't have any solid evidence, just conjecture. None of that will hold up in court. You can't place a solid scenario where Briana and Sondra met and had a confrontation. With that many people at the house, I just don't see someone not noticing. *When* you see my daughter, she will have a lawyer."

Wilkes huffed, standing up sharply. Her face appeared flush as if she was ready to argue, but then her face softened. "I'm sorry this is happening to you and your family. You may not remember, but I was in school with your other daughter, Alexa. I remember Briana as a little girl. But I have to make sure justice is served for a grieving mother and ... two young children who lost their mother."

Amos's stance seemed to shrink a bit, "I know you need to solve this case. I just hope you are looking in the right direction."

"You did this job for a long time, Amos. You know it's imperative that Briana come in and let me question her again. I've been trying to reach her and this doesn't look good for her." She turned to walk towards the door, but then spun around. "I don't want to have to bring either of you in for impeding an investigation but I will."

What? She wanted to throw us in jail.

After Wilkes left, I turned to Amos, my head spinning. "Well, she is something else! Was that a threat?"

Amos rubbed his head, "She's just trying to force our hands like we can tell her where Briana is right now. Even if I did know, I wouldn't tell her. Besides, I need to talk to her before Wilke does."

"I'd say. You know after listening to Wilkes, you

remember your theory about Theo... that he could have confronted Sondra that night?"

"Yes. What about it?"

"Why did they end up letting Theo go?"

Amos walked over to the window and peered out, probably looking for Wilkes to drive away. He turned back around and looked at me. "Pretty much the same deal that Wilkes is trying to put on Briana. That Theo *had* to have seen Sondra. But he too claimed he didn't see her and no one could place him in the backyard. In fact, what Wilkes didn't share and I know is that the death of Sondra happened in the early morning hours, the coroner thinks between midnight and six o'clock on Sunday morning. Theo left the house before midnight." Amos moved away from the window and returned to the couch. "Even I could vouch for that."

I frowned, "You can? How?"

"Remember I went over there to tell Briana to turn the music down. It was about ten o'clock then. Theo was over at the house. What I didn't tell you was I saw him leaving."

I folded my arms, "How do you know he didn't come back?"

"He left because his mother needed him. Apparently she'd been ill and had to be taken to the hospital."

"Okay, that's a pretty solid alibi if people saw him at the hospital."

"Yes, there were several witnesses. Theo is popular in the community. People know who he is."

I sighed, "Who was this witness saying that Sondra was on the property? Why would she show up here? Was she looking for Theo? And..." I thought back to all that I knew about Sondra's last night alive. "Sondra was at the Black

Diamond that night. She left a night of dancing, or whatever, just to show up at Briana's house."

"None of this makes sense. The way she went off on Briana at the coffee shop, the woman was really unhinged. Not that I'm talking about the dead or not acknowledging she was a victim, but it's like you said, Eugeena. She was an abrasive woman." Amos shook his head. "I let myself get caught up in finding J.C. since I knew of his associations."

"Is Wilkes aware of J.C.?"

"I'm sure she is. The circumstances around Briana and this Sondra woman have not helped matters. I just wish I knew where that girl was...I'm trying to be positive, Eugeena. But I have to say in the past few days, I don't feel like I know my own daughter."

"Don't give up on her, Amos. She could just be overwhelmed and running scared. Hopefully, she's listened to your phone messages and the messages from her sister. Most importantly, I know her mom is looking down on her. The one thing you told me about Briana is she never wanted to disappoint her mom."

Amos sighed. "Francine was the glue that held Briana together. She was her baby girl. I'm thankful for us, Eugeena, I really am. But sometimes I wish I could ask Francine what to do about Briana. She always knew exactly what to do."

I placed my hand on Amos's shoulder, and then hugged him. "It will all work out."

I didn't want to offer some cliché or for my words to be in vain. We really needed this all to work out for everyone involved.

Chapter 21

Saturday morning, for once Amos and I slept-in. Detective Wilkes stopping by with her threats yesterday and Briana still missing turned out to be pretty exhausting. The doorbell rang while I was cleaning up dishes from our late breakfast. When I made it to the door, my granddaughter, Keisha, came storming in the house just about knocking me down with a hug.

"Well, look at this surprise." I exclaimed, reaching down to wrap my arms around my granddaughter who was growing so fast.

She had to be a whole inch taller than the last time I saw her.

"Grandma, we wanted to come see you. We were in Columbia all week."

"That's right, your Mama told me you were visiting with Tyric's grandmother. Well, did you have a good time?" I hoped so. Keisha didn't know her dad, but over the years Tyric's dad seemed to have taken to treating her like she was his own.

Speaking of Tyric's dad, Chris's tall frame filled my doorway when I looked up. He had his son on his shoulders. Tyric, who was still going through his terrible twos, was all smiles looking like the spitting image of his father.

"Chris. Nice to see you back in Charleston."

Chris placed Tyric down, "Good to see you too, Ms. Eugeena."

I started to ask him about Leesa, but my daughter showed up practically out-of-breath beside him. "Hey, Mama. Sorry to drop in on you like this, but the kids really wanted to see you today. They missed their Grandma Eugeena."

I grinned, "Come on in. Did y'all already eat?"

"Yes, we stopped by IHOP earlier this morning. Mama, how's Amos doing? Is he here?"

I sighed, "No, he had to ..." I wasn't sure how to answer that question.

"Mama, you okay?" Leesa touched my arm, her eyes concerned.

"Let's sit down. It's been a long week."

The children settled over in the corner with Porgy who was bouncing around, ecstatic to have his two little people come see him.

Leesa sat down on the couch. Chris sidled next to her. I eyed them for a moment, forgetting about my other issues. I didn't want to pry, but they seemed awfully cozy today.

"Mama?" Leesa's insistent voice invaded my thoughts.

"Sorry, I was trying to see if it was a good idea to tell you this. I'm trying to be protective of Amos, but we're all family." I clasped my hands together as though sharing the news was going to pain me. "Amos is out looking for Briana."

Leesa shrieked, "She's missing?"

"I believe she took a break from all that's going on."

Leesa nodded, "I don't blame her, Mama. I've been

talking to some of my classmates and you know I forgot how mean Sondra and her group of friends were to other people. Not to talk bad about the dead, but Sondra was a big bully. Remember the other day you were asking about Yvette? Well, she was just as mean as Sondra."

I nodded, "Yes, I have gathered that. Seems like with Briana being back in town, the past reared its ugly head."

Leesa grimaced, "I saw the video on Facebook. Sondra was going off on Briana. You think she was jealous of Briana hanging out with Theo? Oh and by the way, I did get confirmation that Theo had been pursuing Briana in high school. I learned a lot in the past few days."

I grinned. "Thank you for confirming. I hope I'm not rubbing off on you."

Leesa touched Chris's arm. "Nope, I'm leaving this investigating thing to you and Amos."

Chris smiled at Leesa.

I have not seen these two quite so affectionate in a while. I wonder what has changed?

Chris tore his eyes away from my daughter like he suddenly remembered I was here. "So you really like this detective stuff?"

I shrugged, "Well, I'm not trying to become an official P.I. But if something is happening to my loved ones or friends, I like to get down to the bottom of the situation if I can."

Leesa leaned into Chris, "Hey, Mama, did you know Chris knew Theo a long time ago?"

I actually didn't know much about Chris as I would have liked. I arched my eyebrow turning my attention to my grandson's father. "Did you? How is that possible? Didn't you graduate from Dreher High School? That's in Columbia, right?"

Chris spoke up, "Yes, I moved to Columbia after my parents split. I was born here in Charleston and attended school here up until sixth grade."

"Oh! I didn't know that."

Chris continued, "Yeah, I knew both Theo and Damion. We grew up down the street from one another. Even though I moved from Charleston, I still saw Theo on the football field when our teams played against each other."

Leesa grinned, "Small world, Mama."

Chris agreed, "It really is. I can tell you that Theo has always been a really nice guy. Everyone loved him on and off the field. When I heard what went down last weekend, I had a hard time accepting Theo would have hurt Sondra. I'm glad the cops let him go."

"Taking his mama to the hospital is a pretty solid alibi." Then I remembered from our lunch that Leesa mentioned Chris was related to the owner of the Black Diamond. "Chris, Leesa mentioned you know the owner of the Black Diamond?"

Chris and Leesa exchanged a look. "Yeah, my cousin, Mac Porter, owns the place. May I ask why you want to know, Ms. Eugeena?"

"Sondra started working there a few months ago. I guess your cousin should know her. In fact, she was there last Saturday. I thought it was funny that she would want to hang out at the same place she worked." I leaned forward, "What I really don't understand is why she moved from being at the Black Diamond to ending up at Briana's house?"

Leesa offered, "Maybe she just was in a mood and wanted to start something with Briana. Sondra certainly proved from that video at Sugar Creek Cafe that she didn't have a problem going off in a public place."

"True. Still, that's pretty bold to go to someone's house."

It's on another level of crazy!

Chris nodded, "I agree. But people get tired of a scene and go from party to party. Maybe she didn't know whose house she was going to, especially if she was riding with someone."

I snapped my fingers, "When I talked to Gladys, she said someone picked Sondra up at the house."

Chris offered, "So maybe she didn't have a choice. If her ride was leaving the Black Diamond, she had to go with them."

"Mmm, have you been in the Black Diamond? I'm sure your cousin must have cameras installed."

Chris hesitated, "I've been there once when he opened the place. Yeah, I'm sure he has security, but..."

I eyed him, "But..."

"I love my cousin. Kind of looked up to him when I was younger but you should know that my cousin and I have been on opposite sides of the law. Mac tends to do things that are not legal. Me being a cop and him being family, well, let's just say it's awkward when the family gets together." He leaned forward, a warning written all over his face, "I see where you're going with this, Ms. Eugeena, but I would advise you to stay clear of the Black Diamond and Mac."

Leesa practically jumped off the couch. "Yeah, Mama, don't go too far. Besides, didn't Carmen and I mention to you at lunch the other day that something could have happened at the club?" She side-eyed Chris. "Maybe Chris can work on the case soon since Detective Wilkes is looking in all the wrong directions focusing on poor Briana."

"What?" I was confused. "What are you talking about, Leesa?"

Chris patted Leesa's hands as though he wanted her to calm down, "Everything hasn't gone through yet," he said to her. Then he faced me, "What I think Leesa is trying to tell you, and one of the reasons I came over today is I wanted to let you know I passed the detective exam. There isn't a position open in the Richland County Police Department, but a position has opened up in Charleston. I interviewed this past week."

I clapped my hands together. Well that explained the change in pace with these two. "Oh, that would be wonderful for you to move to Charleston and be near the kids."

Chris looked at Leesa, "Yes, it will be great being close. We needed this change."

Leesa and Chris exchanged looks again. Okay, I knew sparks when I saw them. But before I could say anything Amos entered the house. By the look on his face, something upset him.

"Amos, are you okay?"

He stopped short, noticing Leesa and Chris on the couch. "Hey, I didn't know we had company." He walked over and shook Chris's hand. "How are you doing? It's good to see you again."

Chris stood, towering over Amos, "You too, sir."

Anxious to share the news again, Leesa stated, "Amos, Chris passed his detective exam. And he could be moving to Charleston soon."

Amos smiled, though something still pained him.

"Congratulations, that's wonderful! I knew you could do it."

Amos knew about this.

I didn't even know Chris had those types of aspirations. But with both men being in law enforcement, it made sense they would talk. I appreciated the changes happening in my daughter's life with Chris, but I wanted to know what was bothering Amos. "Amos, is everything okay? We're family." I urged.

Amos sat in his chair. "Yeah, well, I've been looking for someone and I just found out why we weren't able to track him down."

I cocked my head, "Are you referring to ..."

He nodded, "J.C. has been found."

"Found? The way you said it sounds as if he's—"

"Dead." Amos finished my sentence.

Chris and Leesa had been turning their heads looking from Amos to me and back as if they were watching a ping pong match.

Leesa shrieked, "Someone else is dead."

Amos nodded, "The crazy thing? J.C. was killed the same night Sondra had to have been killed. These two people were classmates."

That definitely left any theories of J.C. doing something to Sondra off the table. It also heightened my suspicions more about this group of classmates. I'd lost classmates over the years, but not this young. None of these former students of mine had reached their thirtieth birthday yet.

What was going on with these classmates?

After Leesa and Chris left with the children, I met Amos outside on the front porch. It was still sweltering outside, but the sun was going down. I sat a tray of ice tea on the table between the rocking chairs. The new bamboo fans that Amos helped install earlier this summer gave a bit of breeze as we rocked. Feeling buzzing, I slapped my neck. This lavender scented mosquito concoction I found last summer worked on and off, but it didn't smell horrible, which was why I used it.

Amos guzzled down about half his ice tea before placing it back on the table. "I didn't mention something else to you. I probably said more than I should have in front of Leesa and Chris."

"Oh what else?"

"J.C's body was found near the Black Diamond."

Good thing I hadn't picked up my glass of tea. It would have certainly slipped out of my hand. "You're kidding."

"Nope. My contact in the coroner's office said that J.C's body had been found a day after Sondra's but he hadn't been identified as quickly."

"What does this mean?"

"I don't know, but something happened at the Black Diamond."

My many conversations including the one a few hours ago with Chris spun in my head. "What if Sondra saw something at the Black Diamond? Something having to do with J.C.?"

"That's definitely a possibility."

"Still, how did she get from there to the shed in the back, Amos?"

"That I don't know. I'm fairly certain she arrived here in the neighborhood alive. Whatever happened to cause her death occurred in the backyard next door."

"Well, you know Chris's cousin owns the Black Diamond. Might not hurt to ask your contacts about talking to him. His name is Mac Porter."

Amos swung his head around, his eyes bright. "Really? Mac is related to Chris?"

"Yeah, you know him?"

Amos rubbed his head. "I know Mac Porter is bad news. He's one of those people who manages to have people around him that do bad things, but nothing ever touches him."

"You mean he's never been caught."

Amos chuckled, "You hit the nail on the head with that one, Eugeena."

That made me feel good. For once, it appeared we were getting closer to finding out something crucial. The only lurking question was why?

Why did Sondra and J.C. lose their life on the same night?

Chapter 22

After Leesa's family visit and Amos's shocking news, the rest of the weekend swam by quickly. Monday morning came with still no signs of Briana. I almost wondered if Briana returned to California, deciding her stay in South Carolina needed to end. When she showed up this past April, she never mentioned what happened to her residence in Los Angeles and if her stay was temporary or permanent. Her leaving her guitar still bothered me.

I certainly didn't want to upset Amos, although I could tell he had already wandered in this direction.

Did something happen to Briana? Why else would she stay away without contacting anyone?

Of course she was still seen in town before the weekend talking to Theo. What happened after she met with Theo?

When Amos called Alexa on Sunday night, she claimed her younger sister was known for remaining out of contact for weeks. She suspected Briana had depression and had encouraged her to seek treatment in the past.

That worried me even more. I'd been down this road with Leesa when she'd lost her best friend in high school.

There were things in life that remained out-of-control, but the one thing I knew to do was to pray and that I did.

I also had been neglecting my duties with the summer camp, letting other volunteers substitute for me and today was one of those days I needed to be around children. Their pure innocence did wonders for a person's health.

When I arrived at church, the Brown sisters were already there as expected. Those two had a knack for being on time. Not that I was running late, they just liked to be extra early. I figured they didn't want to miss anything. It surprised me that they didn't say anything to me about the events surrounding my family. I should have known they were just lying in wait for me.

The children had all been fed and were seated at the table munching on hot dogs and chips. After the whirlwind of getting fifteen children settled, I sat in the kitchen feeling aches in parts of my body that I didn't even think I used today. Annie Mae sat down across from me. She managed to keep one eye on the fellowship hall and still state casually, "Gladys will be released from the hospital tomorrow."

"Oh is that so," I responded. "She hadn't been there a week has she? What happened to recovery time?"

"She's ready to get out of there. Get her daughter buried."

Willie Mae almost made me jump. I didn't realize she was behind me. I should have expected the twins to surround and question me the first chance they got.

Well, I had some questions too. Since they liked nosing in other people's business, I was fairly sure they had some knowledge I could use. I decided to plunge into a conversation I knew they were both dying to have. "Did she ever find out who sent her the video?"

Annie Mae faced me with shock on her face. "What video?"

I narrowed my eyes, "You know what video. I'm pretty sure you saw it, both of you. We are too old to be acting coy."

Annie Mae grimaced, "I wasn't going to mention it."

"Me neither," Willie Mae agreed.

I looked from one sister to the other. "Really? I still want to know who took it and how it ended up on Facebook."

"That is curious. Now that you mention it, Gladys was actually wondering the same thing. She mentioned that she isn't on Facebook that much and that someone sent it to her phone." Annie Mae shrugged, "She didn't seem to recognize the phone number."

Willie Mae scoffed, "She was probably embarrassed to see her daughter acting like that in public. That was just like Sondra."

Annie Mae grunted her agreement, "That girl got her meanness from her mama."

Now these two sisters were known for not being the nicest people themselves. And the fact that they were accusing someone else of being mean had me shaking my head.

I wanted to ask more about Gladys, but Annie Mae stood from her seat, her attention riveted on somebody's child. "That's enough of that! You finish your food."

I looked to see who Annie Mae was fussing at and realized the victim, or culprit according to Annie Mae, was Sondra's son. The little boy stuck his lip out and stared back in quiet defiance.

"Mmm, that one right there is just like his mama and grandmama. He doesn't take after his dad at all."

I frowned, "Are you still looking after Sondra's kids?"

Willie Mae appeared quietly beside me. "Yes. It's all so sad. I feel bad for them."

"That was awfully nice of you." Since Annie Mae mentioned Theo, I asked, "Has their dad asked about them?"

Willie Mae nodded, "Oh yeah, he's been by to see them." She dropped her voice, "I have a feeling he's going to want custody of the kids. Being the biological dad, he will probably get it too." There was a slight smile on Willie Mae's face. She wasn't a smiling woman. "It's been kind of nice to have children around the house. The little girl kind of reminds me of Pat at her age."

I knew Willie Mae missed her daughter. I responded, "I'm glad you were able to step in and help. I'm sure Gladys appreciates it too." I thought for a moment. "Might be good for Theo to take in his own kids. Gladys can't handle those two children with her heart condition."

Annie Mae turned around, "We wondered the same thing, but apparently she's determined to hang on to her grandkids. Theo is going to have a fight on his hands. Gladys has even lined up some help from our cousin's girl."

I frowned, "Who's your cousin?"

Annie Mae, "You may remember her. Agnes Hunt. Her daughter, Charlene was a friend of Sondra. Agnes passed on a few years ago but we try to keep up with Charlene when we can."

My ears perked up. "Charlene? Yeah, I know her. Wow, that's awfully nice of her to offer to help Gladys."

Awfully nice and suspicious. What was that girl doing?

"Did you two know Charlene was with Sondra the same night she'd been killed? They were together at that Black Diamond night club."

The twins exchanged a look between themselves, one that I couldn't read.

I waited for them to respond, but neither said a word which I found to be peculiar. "I saw Charlene last week and apparently the two girls hadn't been in touch for some time, maybe even since high school. I gathered it had something to do with Yvette."

This time both twins eyed me and for once Willie Mae's wondering eye was looking directly at me. I know I'd stepped into their family business, but these two didn't exactly resist being in my business.

Willie Mae asked, "What do you know about Yvette?"

"Not much. I had Charlene in my social studies class, but I wasn't aware of her twin until recently. I vaguely remembered Yvette getting shot."

"Mmmmm." Annie Mae began to rock. "That was an awful time for the family, especially Agnes. She shut down. Charlene was very dependent on her twin. Her mama wasn't really paying attention to her. For some reason, Agnes doted on Yvette a bit more."

Willie Mae nodded, "Poor Charlene got a little lost after that. She stopped talking to a lot of people. I don't think Sondra was the only one. Charlene managed to get mixed in with the wrong crowd and did drugs for a while. It's sad, but Agnes gave up on her own daughter."

Annie Mae added, "Yeah, it wasn't until after her mother died that Charlene got clean. Our Pat helped her get into rehab. "

"I didn't realize Charlene had been through so much. I imagine it was awfully hard to lose her twin and then have her mother checked out in a way too."

Willie Mae sighed, "Yeah, that girl hasn't always had it together, but she's a sweet girl. Sweeter than her sister. Yvette and Sondra, now those were a force. Both of them were pretty girls and they let it go to their heads. Charlene was definitely a third wheel."

I frowned, "Is Gladys aware of Charlene's history? Why do you think she's trusting her to help with the kids?"

Annie Mae shrugged, "I don't know, but last week when we visited Gladys in the hospital, we ran into Charlene. She seemed almost as distraught as Gladys."

I'd never had a chance to talk to Charlene since seeing her at the auto shop last week. That encounter had struck me as odd, and the more I learned about her the more something nagged me.

Before I could think to ask anything else about Charlene, a ping sound came from my phone. I frowned. That wasn't the usual tone I heard for a text. When I reached in my purse for my phone I realized it was the Simple Security app. Amos had shown me how to use the app and I found myself looking at the cameras over the weekend. I used it to spy on Porgy while he was outside. Nothing special other than watching him chase a squirrel. I was starting to believe it was the same squirrel taunting my dog.

I opened the app wondering if Amos had ordered a package or something. I knew I didn't. There were some weeks where I clicked that Amazon button way too much. I was too preoccupied the past few weeks to be shopping.

When I saw who was on the camera, I gasped.

Both the twins who had started cleaning up the kitchen turned around to look at me.

"Eugeena, you okay?" Annie Mae asked.

I couldn't answer if I wanted to, my mouth was tongue-tied. I was too shocked to see the young woman's face peering at my front door.

Briana was back. Girl, where have you been?

Chapter 23

I hurried home as quick as I could. I sent a text to Amos to let him know his daughter had returned. I just hope she remained in place until he arrived. I practically skidded into the driveway so if my plan was to surprise her, I'm sure she had either heard or seen me coming. Once I parked the Camry, I sat for a few minutes.

A sistah needed to catch her breath and think for a minute!

From the moment I saw Briana's face on the security app, I went into overdrive. I'm not sure what I thought I could do or even say to her. I just felt the urge to make sure she was okay.

After finally coming to some resemblance of a plan, I got out of my car and decided to go in my house first. I'm sure Porgy could use a walk in the yard being cooped up the past few hours. As I watched my dog tear around the yard, I looked over in the other yard. Most of the houses on my street had a bit of privacy usually by a fence or shrubbery. Years ago, Ralph had a wooden fence installed all around the yard. When the boys were young and living at home, Ralph and the boys would wash down the fence as well as the deck that was eventually added. Then they stained it to protect it from the sun.

I stared over that fence now, for some reason noticing the shed for the first time. I'm sure I'd seen it before, but it really stood out to me. Probably because over a week ago a real dead body had been found.

A body that Briana was being accused of placing there. What struck me and I'm not sure why it didn't occur to me before was how much effort it would have been to drag what had to be *dead* weight into the shed.

Briana had her mother's frame, which was much lighter and slimmer than mine. She wasn't skinny, but she didn't strike me as one who could heft a lot of weight. Briana wasn't short, but slightly taller than my 5'4 frame.

I finally got Porgy back inside and headed over to the house. A few moments later, Briana peeked her head out. As I suspected she was not happy to see me.

The grimace on her face disappeared as quickly as it appeared. In its place was a more haggard look as if the child hadn't slept in a while.

"Are you okay?" I peered at her. "I saw you were home and wondered if we could talk."

"Sure," Briana left the door open and I followed her inside.

Well, at last she didn't close the door in my face.

I noticed the place looked a bit cleaner than it did the last time.

Briana turned around, her arms were wrapped around her similar to the way they were the night Sondra's body was found.

"I'm really here to see if you are alright. I'm sure your dad has been in touch with you."

"Yes, him and my sister have been blowing up my phone."

"I'm sure Detective Wilkes has too."

Fear flashed in Briana's eyes. "Is she going to arrest me?"

"I don't think she has anything on you other than some circumstantial stuff like the video."

Briana dropped down on the couch. "I can't believe someone recorded that. I was doing my job. I wasn't crazy about the job at first, but it was cool hanging around Fay and Jocelyn at the cafe. I do love coffee."

I had to smile at that. "Well, that's something we both have in common." I took it upon myself to sit across from her. "Briana, if you knew who Sondra was in the first place, why did you pretend you didn't?"

Her eyes flashed and then watered, "I wasn't pretending. I couldn't process what I was seeing. I didn't understand what or how a dead body was in my yard."

"That's understandable. You were in shock."

Briana's bottom lip trembled, "When I heard you and my dad talking about her in the kitchen, it started to occur to me that I could get blamed for her death." She threw her hands up as if all was lost. "Just my luck, being blamed for killing somebody I didn't even know was in my house. Somebody who hated me for such stupid reasons."

"Are you sure you never saw her Saturday night? Detective Wilkes is convinced Sondra showed up to start trouble with you and Theo."

Briana shook her head, "No. I never saw her and neither did Theo. Besides, he left the party early when his mom called. She wasn't feeling good. I was too busy trying to be the hostess most of the night. I served food, drinks and even sang a couple of songs." Briana stared off into space, "I will say after Theo left, everyone else seemed ready to go. The party was over probably forty-five minutes after he left. I was exhausted and went to bed."

I nodded. "Well, what's even more crazy is she was at

the Black Diamond. That's like what, ten miles from Sugar Creek? I can't get why she would come all the way here? Certainly the woman wasn't that vindictive to pick a fight with someone in their own house? And if you never saw her, then I'm wondering if Sondra came here not realizing this is where you lived?"

Briana stared off into space as if her mind was trapped by a dark memory. "Theo told me Sondra had been trying to get back together. He said he made the mistake of spending time with her. He was doing it because he thought it would make his kids happy, but he finally gave up because she was so demanding. She never had anything good to say about him. He told me he got into a huge argument with her before Christmas and that he only wanted to co-parent with her."

"Before Christmas. That was over seven months ago. Sounds like Sondra never took the hint."

Briana rolled her eyes, "Sondra was never a person who understood the word no."

"I imagine her friend was the same way."

Briana frowned, "Who?"

"Yvette."

Briana bristled as if an electric current had stung her. "You know about her?"

"I've heard a lot I didn't know in the past week."

Briana dropped her head in her hands. "I can't believe all this is happening. I left California to come home for some peace. You would think after all this time life would be different. High school was almost a decade ago."

"I'm sorry. Some people never quite grow up from the high school experience." Since I was curious, I changed the subject and asked, "Have you ever been to the Black Diamond?"

Briana lifted her head from her hands. "Yeah, I had a gig there last month. It was my first paying gig since being in South Carolina. It's not the most classy place, but I missed being in front of an audience. The stage was a pretty decent size and I liked the band."

"Did you know Sondra worked there?"

Briana's eyes grew wide, "No, I didn't know that."

I nodded, "I was trying to figure out how she knew you were back in town. Charleston isn't exactly a small town, and Sondra didn't live here in Sugar Creek."

Briana shrugged, "I doubt Theo would have said something to her. He was keeping contact to a minimum with her, only to pick up the kids. I know he said that lately her mother was giving him trouble about picking up the kids."

"Gladys? I would think she would want the father in their lives." I thought back to my earlier conversation with the Brown twins. Like mother, like daughter, both Gladys and Sondra seemed to have a mean streak in them. They also mentioned Gladys was determined to keep her grandchildren despite her health condition. She was even bringing in help.

"Briana, what do you know about Charlene?"

Briana frowned, "Charlene Hunt? She was Yvette's sister. I remember her being shy and wanting to fit in. To be honest, we both were probably a lot alike, but Charlene had her sister and Sondra." Suddenly Briana's face went rigid as she stared off again. "Oh no."

"What? Are you remembering something?"

"Charlene was here at the house."

Emotions warred in my body as some of my questions were being confirmed. "When was this?"

"Last Saturday. I saw her talking to Damion. At first, I

didn't recognize her, but then I remembered she came to the cafe with Sondra. She's always been skinny, but she seemed like she hadn't been well."

I didn't have a good feeling about this. "She's apparently had a hard time since her sister's death. Do you know what time you saw Charlene?"

"I don't remember the time. I know she showed up after Theo left. Damion came over looking for his brother, but Theo had already left to check on his mom. "

"You're sure you didn't notice Sondra?"

"I'm positive! You don't believe me?" Briana's voice rose in accusation.

"No. I believe you did nothing wrong, Briana. I'm on your side here. What I'm trying to say is when I talked to Charlene last week, she claimed Sondra was with her. That they had met at the Black Diamond. I have a feeling they were riding together in the same car."

Briana shook her head, "This doesn't make sense. I had quite a few people over that night, but I saw everyone's face. I may not have known all of them. Some people brought guests. I can't imagine that I would have missed Sondra."

"Especially after she confronted you at Sugar Creek Cafe."

Briana grew quiet and hung her head. When she looked up, unshed tears clung to her lashes. "I'm going to get blamed for all of this no matter what. People are going to assume the same thing they did years ago. That I somehow got back at a person who'd been harassing me."

I didn't have time to agree or disagree. The doorbell rang.

I reached for my phone and switched on the security app. "Oh no."

"What? What are you looking at on your phone?" Briana asked.

"The camera for this house. While you were gone, your dad had Simply Security cameras installed. You have a visitor." I turned the phone around so Briana could see the display.

Briana jumped up from the couch, "What am I going to do?"

I held up a finger, "First, let me call your father. Second, when we answer the door, you are not to say anything until your dad gets you a lawyer."

I pressed the speed dial for Amos's phone.

He answered on the second ring. "Eugeena, I'm almost there."

"You better hurry and I hope you secured that lawyer for Briana. Detective Wilkes is at the door right now." The doorbell rang again, this time long and hard. I added, "Wilkes sounds like she's ready to break the door down."

"Hold tight, I'm right around the corner."

After he hung up, I faced Briana, "Your father is on the way. You ready?"

"I don't think I have a choice."

When I opened the door, Detective Wilkes' flushed face glared through the screen door at us. "Thank you for finally answering the door."

"We didn't mean to make you wait."

"Can we come in?"

I observed behind Wilkes. She didn't come alone today. Not one, but two deputies stood behind her.

What's all of this? Where is Amos?

Once inside, Wilkes zoned in on Briana. "Nice to finally see you again, Ms. Jones. I thought you might have skipped town after I specifically told you not to."

It occurred to me that I still had no idea where Briana had gone. It made sense that the detective would have asked her not to leave town. Briana sure did know how to make things harder on herself. I hoped Amos would show up soon because I was losing ground with knowing what to do with Wilkes here.

I stepped up beside Briana. "Detective Wilkes, are you here to ask Briana questions?"

"I have questions, but I need Briana to come with me down to the station." One of the deputies stepped forward while reaching for handcuffs.

Briana shrank back, "You're arresting me?"

The deputy glanced over his shoulder at Detective Wilkes as though he needed confirmation, "Yes, ma'am."

Briana stared at me as if I could stop this from happening. I was just as shocked that Wilkes was doing this.

As the detective began reading Briana her rights, Amos burst through the door. "What's going on? Do you have an arrest warrant?

Wilkes stopped mid-sentence and held up her hand, "Mr. Jones, please, I'm doing my job."

He stated, "Are you, because you don't have anything substantial to be arresting my daughter?"

"Yes, we do. A witness has come forward. I'm going to ask you again, out of respect, to let me do my job or I will have to take you to the station too."

I thought to myself, *Who would come forward now? What did they see?* I was not buying that Detective Wilkes supposedly had a witness now. I smelled something fishy going on and I didn't like it. Somebody was deliberately playing with Briana's life, setting Amos's child as the killer.

My husband glared at the petite detective like he didn't believe her either. He spouted out instructions to Briana. "Don't you say a word. I will be there with your lawyer."

I felt so helpless watching them walk Briana outside towards the police car. Amos took off towards his truck to be there at the station with Briana.

I glanced around and found several neighbors, including Louise, watching as Briana was placed in the back of the car. She waved at me. I waved back, but I would get with Louise later.

Though the situation seemed to be spiraling out-of-control, I wasn't discouraged. I was going to find this witness. I had a sneaky suspicion, I knew who was behind all of this madness.

Chapter 24

I knew there was one person who kept coming up over and over again. Charlene Hunt. I needed to find her. I'm not sure what I was going to do when I found her. It's not like you can make a person talk. And there was the maddening thought racing through my mind.

What if she was the killer?

I'd made mistakes in the past not realizing I was walking into crazy.

My mind kept stumbling back to a teenage girl I once knew and even the young woman who approached me last week. Timidity struck me as the main quality that described Charlene. But anyone could strike out when pushed to the edge. Sondra was one of those kinds of people who had no problem pushing people's buttons.

What kept bothering me was why all of a sudden did Charlene and Sondra want to rekindle their friendship? Who was the initiator? One thing was for sure, Sondra ended up dead and I absolutely believed it was set off by events that happened last Saturday night at the Black Diamond.

Events that also resulted in someone else's death.

J.C.

I knew all these individuals were in the same class, but did they all run into each other at the Black Diamond?

Charlene admitted to me without me asking her that she had been with Sondra. It made sense to me that she more than likely had to be this so-called witness. But a witness to what? Surely if you saw someone harm your friend, you would have called the police on them right there, not over a week later.

Why wait all this time to come forward?

I didn't know for sure if I was barking up the wrong tree, but I wanted face time with Charlene for myself. The woman came up to me last week as if she had something to say. I believed she would talk to me. Maybe it had something to do with me being her former teacher.

I set off down the street to my destination since it was in walking distance. I had built up enough stress that I needed the movement. The sun was bearing down on me as I walked, but I didn't mind.

I was on a mission.

They must have seen me coming because before I could ring the doorbell Annie Mae was sticking her head out the door. "Eugeena, what's going on?"

I thought I would be the one asking the questions.

I stopped in front of the door, placing my hands on my hips. By this time I was huffing and puffing, more than just from the short, brisk walk in the hot sun. "I'm pretty sure you saw. The police came and took Briana away."

Willie Mae peered from behind her sister, "So she did do it?"

"No, she didn't!" I raised my hands in the air.

Annie Mae grimaced, "No need to make a scene. It seemed like the police must have found something. Come on in here! You're letting our air out."

I stepped inside the Brown sisters' living room, welcoming the cool air. Though the twins and I see each other every week, between summer camp and church on Sunday, we didn't often visit each other's home. The sisters kept their place super tidy. They ran a tight ship on the usher board and didn't play with the children we served at church. No surprises about their no frills, basic living setup.

"Do you want something to drink, Eugeena? We don't serve that kind of drink."

I rolled my eyes. "Are you trying to be funny, Willie Mae? You know I don't drink alcohol. If you have some water that would be fine."

Annie Mae held out her arm, "Why don't you have a seat? You know we were wondering why you took off from the church so fast earlier today. You look tired."

"Tired and confused." I took the bottled water Willie Mae handed me, "Thank you. I appreciate this." I took a swig of water, which was exactly what I needed. I didn't realize I was this parched. It was then that I glanced out to their side yard and noticed the twins were not alone. Sondra's kids were outside playing. I frowned, "I thought the kids were going home with Gladys."

Willie Mae turned around to look out the window, returning her attention back to me, her shoulders slumped. "She was supposed to pick them up at the church."

I frowned, "I see. Well, have you heard from her? It's probably not a good idea that she handles the kids on her own with her condition."

Annie Mae answered, "We've called her house two times and left a message. Once before leaving the church.

We decided to just bring the kids back with us. They've been staying with us this long now."

Willie Mae piped up, "If Gladys doesn't show up soon, we thought about calling the children's father. Theo has been calling us and asking if we needed anything. He is really a good man, so I don't know why he doesn't have more custody of the kids anyway. Gladys fussed about him so much, but he seemed to be perfectly fine with stepping up."

I really didn't want to get off topic, but I realized after sitting in the twins' living room that I needed to ask questions about one of their own relatives. No matter how crazy a family member could be, blood was blood. If I pressed the twins more about Charlene, they could decide to shut down all together.

I was desperate knowing that poor Briana could be thrown in jail for something she didn't do. Then I recalled something Willie Mae said. "You know last week when we were talking about the party Briana had, you mentioned you looked out to see who was in the neighborhood."

Willie Mae eyed me. "Yes, why?"

"Did you happen to see who was coming in and out of the house? Did the police question you at all?"

Willie Mae shook her head. "No, if the cops came by our house, neither one of us talked to them."

"But did you see anything?"

Annie Mae leaned forward, "I'm sure Willie Mae didn't see anything, though she tried looking. Her eyes are not the best."

Willie Mae snapped at her sister, "There is nothing wrong with my eyes."

Annie Mae rolled her eyes, "You know you've been putting off going to the ophthalmologist for years. She peeks out the window, but I doubt she can see farther than her face."

Willie Mae argued, "You don't know that."

Okay, these two were giving me a headache.

"Ladies, I'm trying to see if you saw Charlene. It seemed like you mentioned you knew the people over there.

Annie Mae frowned, "Why are you asking about Charlene again? We talked about her earlier? The child wouldn't harm a fly."

I sighed, "I'm not saying she would, but she was out with Sondra that night. She had to have seen what happened. The detective is claiming to have a witness now."

Both twins exclaimed, "Witness?"

"Yes, someone has felt compelled to come forward. The only person who I could think to be this witness has to be Charlene. She and Sondra were together most of the night. I want to know what she knows."

"So, what are you asking us, Eugeena?"

"How do I find her?"

The twins exchanged looks again, both of them looking weary at my request.

"Y'all, I just want to know what happened. I could feel Charlene holding back on something when I saw her last week."

"Charlene has been through enough. I don't know if we should be letting you bother her." Annie Mae said, shaking her head.

Willie Mae observed me for a moment before getting up to go to another room.

Annie Mae frowned, "Willie Mae, what are you doing?"

Her sister showed up with a notebook and pencil in her

hand. She scribbled on it and handed it over to me. "Here is her address."

I reached for the piece of paper stating my thanks.

Annie Mae's eyes opened in shock, "Why did you give Eugeena the girl's address?"

Willie Mae turned to her sister. "You remember when Pat was trying to help Charlene?"

"Help with what?" I asked. Willie Mae didn't talk about Pat much. Her daughter's death had been too painful. After a long battle with drugs, Pat found God and went back to school for her nursing degree. She was doing so well when tragedy struck. I found it touching and alarming all at the same time that she was sharing something about Pat.

Willie Mae turned to me, "After Pat got out of rehab years ago, she worked to mentor young people. It was Pat who found Charlene and helped her get on the right track. I remember Pat saying that when Charlene was high that she turned aggressive. It was so disturbing to see because she's such a sweet and quiet person."

Annie Mae shook her head, "What are you saying?" Annie Mae turned to me, "Are you looking for Charlene because you think she did something?"

I shrugged, "I'm not accusing anyone, but Charlene was with Sondra. Somehow the police are focused on Briana because of some beef between her and Sondra. I just think they're not even bothering to see all angles from that night. They just want to wrap up a case. My gut says Charlene knows something. And..." I caught my breath. "Years ago, Charlene's sister got into it with Briana. Yvette was killed and suspicion was thrown Briana's way back then too. You said Charlene was never the same. I imagine the girl has a lot of anger."

I stopped talking because Sondra's kids burst inside the house. I'd almost forgotten they were outside playing.

The young boy, looking like a young version of Theo asked, "Has grandma called yet? We really want to see her."

Willie Mae soothed, "No, not yet."

I decided it was time for me to leave, there was obvious tension between the two sisters now and I felt guilty for causing it. "Ladies, I've overstayed. Look, I can go by to check on Gladys. Sounds like she may need a house call. I'll let you know what's going on."

As I returned to my house I decided I better call Amos. He must have been really tied up at the station. I almost hung up the phone instead of waiting for his voicemail.

Amos came on, his voice raspy. "Hey, Eugeena."

"Amos, you don't sound too good. How are things going?"

"Not well, but they could be worse. Barnaby is here and he's doing his best to get some answers from Detective Wilkes."

"Did you find out about the witness?"

"Not yet."

"I have an idea who it may be."

"You do, who?"

"Remember Charlene Hunt was with Sondra. Somebody picked up Sondra from her mother's house. They all went to the Black Diamond. As you know something happened there that may have resulted in J.C.'s death. Before Wilkes arrived, Briana remembered seeing Charlene. Charlene and Sondra had to arrive together."

Amos was quiet for a moment. "You think Charlene is this witness?"

"I'm guessing. She's related to the Brown sisters who gave me her address."

Amos responded, "You're not going over there."

"Not now, but I do want to check on Gladys."

"Why, I thought she didn't react very well to you last week? Is it a good idea for you to be going to see her either?"

I sighed, "Probably not, but I believe Gladys is too trusting of Charlene. The girl has had some problems."

"Everybody has problems, Eugeena."

"I know, I know. Look, I will be fine. I just need Gladys to think about this more. I know she's grieving, but there were other people over at Brianna's that had access to Sondra."

Amos sighed, "I really need to be here for Briana. I don't need to be worrying about you, Eugeena."

"I'm going to be just fine. All Gladys can do is yell at me again. I have to try to reach out to her. I'm telling you something is up with this girl. I want to know when Sondra actually started hanging out with Charlene. Last Saturday wasn't the first time. We know that because the previous Monday, they were together at Sugar Creek Cafe."

"Be careful, Eugeena. If you feel like you need to reach out to Gladys fine, but don't approach Charlene if you have all these suspicions. I've seen how your gut pans out and usually you are on the right track."

"I will keep you updated. Okay? Tell Briana I'm praying for her. I love you, Amos."

"I love you too, Eugeena."

I hung up the phone. Amos and I weren't expressive people that often. Something about his concern set me on the edge and I wanted him to know that I loved him for it.

I took in a deep breath, already feeling the tension building from what I was about to do. My last conversation with Gladys wasn't a good one but I needed to do my part to get Briana out of this situation. Though Sondra was the victim, I couldn't help but wonder if we'd be in this predicament if she'd stayed away from the house.

Chapter 25

It had only been a week since I visited Gladys's home. So much had happened. That day Gladys was worried about her daughter not returning home and by the end of the day she found out she'd never see Sondra again. At least not on this side of the earth. I prayed mother and daughter would be united again in another time.

When I arrived, I walked up to Gladys's doorway. I could hear her television booming through the window. I rang the doorbell and stood on the steps waiting for her to answer. It seemed odd that she wouldn't have come to pick up her grandkids if she was home.

Unless...

I'm not one to peek inside people's windows. That's not something I would want someone to do to me, but Gladys had a heart attack just last week. She shouldn't have been out and from my knowledge her doctor should have had her going for some kind of rehab. It wasn't a major heart attack, but it still took her down, at a minimum she should have been resting.

I leaned over and looked inside the window pane next to the door. The hallway was actually pretty dim except there was a light coming from down the hall. I'd only been to Gladys's house that one time last week. I've never done more than have a conversation with her at church over the years. Like most folks, we headed to our own lives after church services and saw each other again the following Sunday.

I wondered if the light was coming from a room, maybe a downstairs bedroom. I laid my finger on the doorbell and rang it again, this time longer. As I rang the bell, I continued to look inside the window pane. I stepped to the side.

Nothing.

Maybe Glady just left the light on. I did that sometimes or at least until Amos and I got married. When I lived in the house alone, it helped to have an extra light on. The house didn't feel so lonely.

I took one more look and just as I was about to turn, movement caught my eye.

Was that a shadow?

I drew closer to the window pane. There was something like a shadow on the opposite wall. Was Gladys in that room ignoring the doorbell?

I mean I've been known to do that too.

The last thing I hated at this time of the day, well anytime of the day, was someone at my door soliciting. Made me more grateful that Amos went ahead and got the security app. I liked the idea that I could really ignore the doorbell now if it wasn't someone who needed to be at my door anyway.

I waited, feeling the hot rays of the sun bearing down on my neck and back.

Something wasn't right.

Either it was my eyes playing tricks on me, or there was

definitely someone moving in the room lighting the hallway.

There are moments when you do something and you don't realize you're being led. That's what I felt like when I touched Gladys's doorknob. In this day and age, people simply didn't leave their doors open like they did when I was a little girl. The crime rate here in Charleston and the way of the world over the years garnered the need for caution.

To my surprise, Gladys's doorknob turned and her door opened. I was so shocked, I gripped the doorknob in pure fear, conscious of my heart rate speeding up. Then I focused and took my hands off the knob to study the lock. I didn't know anything about picking locks other than what I saw on television, but someone had been messing with this lock for sure.

On the weekend, I was known for finding one of those silly Lifetime movies where the character is about to walk into a place. As the viewer, I could see the danger, usually the camera panned to the woman on the screen making it seem like someone was watching her from the shadows. Eventually that person snuck up and attacked the woman. I looked over my shoulder seeing no one on the street or even in front of Gladys's house.

Nope, no one was going to surprise me from behind. But who was inside?

I could almost hear Amos's words from less than an hour ago.

Be careful, Eugeena.

I took a breath and stepped inside, attempting to reign in my imagination. Once inside, I closed the front door behind me, hoping this wasn't classified as breaking and entering. The last thing I needed to be doing was get arrested too. As far as I was concerned my reasons for entering were legitimate. I was checking on a woman who had a heart attack last week and no one had heard from her. And the door was open.

"Gladys," I called out. "Are you okay? Annie Mae and Willie Mae have been trying to reach you. They are keeping the kids at their house."

Silence met me.

I should have turned around, but that movement earlier had me curious. I wasn't trying to hear that old saying right now. Yeah, that one about curiosity killed the ...

I wasn't a four-legged creature but I would beat myself up later if something had happened to Gladys and I didn't do everything in my power to help. For all I knew, that movement could have been her reaching out for help.

A verse came to mind and I prayed.

God, you are my protector. This is my moment to be strong and courageous because you said you would never leave me nor forsake me. I need to know Gladys is alright. Those children don't need any more turmoil in their lives.

I made my way down the hall practically on my toes. That was quite a feat since I couldn't recall ever having to sneak around like this.

I froze, feeling iciness crawl down my spine.

What was that noise?

I listened. Nope, nothing.

Then, a deep moan penetrated my ears causing my heart to leap again in my chest. I propelled myself to move forward though I wanted to turn and run for the door. When I peered around the doorframe, the first thing I saw was Gladys slumped down the wall. It appeared to be a bedroom, but I didn't know if it was her bedroom or her deceased daughter's.

I entered, "Gladys, are you okay?"

Her eyes fluttered, but didn't focus on me. The closer I got to her, I thought perhaps she had fallen. Until... I stepped closer.

There was a gash on her head.

"Did you fall and hit your head, Gladys?"

Gladys moaned again.

I reached for my phone, which thank goodness I had slipped into my pocket before I got out of the car. I typed in the passcode. "Hold on, I will get some help."

"No, you won't be calling nobody."

I froze, my finger stalled over the phone app.

Someone else was here.

My mind flashed to the door lock. Someone had picked their way in here. I glanced over at Gladys again, whose eyes now focused on someone behind me.

"Turn around."

The voice was familiar.

I turned slowly, wondering why I didn't listen to Amos's warnings. And how didn't I see this coming. Sadly, this wasn't the first time seeing a gun up close, but the last person I expected to see was the person holding it.

At least Amos knows where to look for my body.

I let my arm drop to the side, but I had no intentions of letting go of my phone.

If something happened to me, I wanted someone to know who did it.

Chapter 26

I should have been scared, but instead I was mad. Mad that I'd focused my attention on the wrong person. I peeked at Gladys again, wondering if I could persuade the large figure blocking the doorway with reason. Gladys appeared to be fading fast. There was no telling how bad she was hurt since she was already in a weakened state. The woman should have stayed in the hospital.

I faced the figure in front of me, standing to my full height and with my sternest voice I asked, "Is this really necessary? Did you do this to Gladys? This woman is your mama's age. What were you thinking?"

Damion stepped forward out of the shadows of the hallway. He appeared to be sweaty, his eyes glassy. "She deserved it. Just like her daughter deserved to die. People like them just bring trouble to other people." He tipped his head towards Gladys. "This one in particular liked to pretend like she was all good and Christian."

I thought back to my conversation with Damion last week. He wasn't shy about expressing his hatred for Sondra. He also admitted to being protective of Charlene.

Had the two been working together?

"Did you kill Sondra, Damion? I thought you were

Briana's friend. You're going to let her go down for something she didn't do. I don't understand."

I knew I shouldn't agitate Damion, but I had to know. That was me all the way, didn't know when to stop even with a gun pointed at me.

Damion shuffled forward. I watched his face shift from hard to indecision, as if for a slight second he wasn't sure what he was doing. "I'm sorry about Briana. None of that was supposed to happen. I was going to fix everything."

I guessed, "You weren't expecting Briana to go to the shed and find the body."

"After Theo left, the party was winding down anyway." Damion snorted, "Theo has always been the life of the party. He left in time too. Because Sondra showed up, and she'd been drinking. I asked Charlene why she brought her to the house. I was surprised at her. Charlene is sweet, but when she got around the wrong people, they influenced her. I could tell Charlene was ripe to see Sondra do something."

I listened. Now this was what had my focus. I felt the whole time there was some kind of dynamic going on between Sondra and Charlene for them to even have the nerve to show up at Briana's home.

He glanced away, his arm lowering the gun only slightly. The memory from that night must have caught his attention, for that I was grateful because I still had my phone in my hand. I placed my hands behind my back fumbling with the phone. If only I could figure out what button to touch. Under favorites, I knew Amos's number was first. If only my hands could move that nimbly. It's not like I had young hands anymore, some days I felt the pangs of arthritis.

Hands don't fail me now!

Damion interrupted my concentration, "It happened so fast. Sondra was spouting off like she always does. Threatening to make sure my brother never sees his kids."

I frowned, still trying to figure out what I was pressing. A few weeks ago Leesa fussed at me about keeping the phone sounds so loud. From that conversation, I'd turned down the sound levels on the clicks. I hoped they were low enough that Damion couldn't hear. I'd also just typed in my passcode, and I knew I didn't have but maybe five minutes before the phone locked again.

I forced myself to multitask, focus on Damion and the phone, "Why would she do that? It's my understanding that Theo is an upstanding citizen, he runs a reputable business. If anyone is more qualified to have custody of the kids, I would think it would be Theo."

"Yeah, you right he should, but Sondra holds stuff over people. Theo had my back a few times. Stuff he would have never done. I don't know how Sondra found out what she knew, but she made sure to use it against Theo."

I hoped I was pressing the right thing. I heaved in a breath and continued to engage with Damion. "I remember Sondra being overly aggressive and saying things to people that were upsetting."

I probably shouldn't have been talking, but I wanted to appear to be trying to understand his side even though I really didn't. I slipped the phone back into the pocket of my sundress.

He nodded his head, his eyes distant. "Yeah, that was her style. All up in somebody's face calling herself trying to threaten someone. That woman never had any sense."

"She was being ugly to you. You couldn't take it anymore. I get it. You shoved her away. The shove was a bit too hard. She fell and hit her head. But why didn't you call for help? It was still an accident. She was in your face and you just pushed her away."

Damion scoffed, "With my record, cops are always looking for a way to put me back in jail. She wasn't moving. I could tell something was wrong and I sure wasn't about to go down because of *her*."

"I see. But why is there a witness trying to put this all on Briana? That's not right, Damion."

Damion sighed, "I had nothing to do with that. Charlene has always blamed Briana for her sister's death. And she's probably trying to keep the cops off me."

"You two protect each other, I see."

Damion had the gun lowered now as well as his head. I still wasn't planning any quick movements and I prayed I had pressed something that allowed someone to hear this conversation.

"She should blame me."

"What?"

"Charlene should blame me. I was talking to Yvette that night. We were shooting the breeze, laughing and then I saw the car coming. Actually, I heard it first. I recognized the Mustang's engine. I knew who was in the car because I was there when they worked on that car. I knew they were coming for me."

I sucked in a breath, "The person who shot Yvette? They were after you?"

"Yeah, I dived down. I knew it was coming. None of the bullets hit me. I shouted to Yvette, 'Get down, get down.' She had this confused look on her face because we were just laughing so hard. I think she thought I was playing. Then I saw the bullets rip into her. The look on her face, I will never forget it."

Damion was breathing hard like he was trying to push

the pain back, "Charlene doesn't look or act like her sister, but I know that was her twin. They were close. I saw what Yvette's death did to her and her family. I tried to protect her over the years since I couldn't protect her sister."

There was quiet between us for what seemed like a long time. It was a lot to process. I was also listening hard for some police sirens or something.

I checked on Gladys. Her eyes were closed and she didn't appear to be moving. "That doesn't explain why you're messing with an old woman. She just had a heart attack, Damion. We have to get her to a hospital."

He looked down at Gladys as if he'd just remembered she was there. "No. She wasn't supposed to be here. I thought she was still in the hospital."

I narrowed my eyes. "Then, why did you come here?"

The hardness returned to his eyes as he focused on me. "I like you, Mrs. Patterson. I meant it when I said I liked your class." His voice took on a menacing tone, "But you ask too many questions. You shouldn't be here either."

I sucked in a breath as fear crept all over my body. From what I could gather, Damion had every intention of coming into this house and apparently was surprised by Gladys returning home. My guess was that Gladys saw him. Either she set off towards him or was trying to run away from him. Either way, Damion must have shoved her in a similar way he did to her daughter over a week ago.

You would think the man paid attention to his own strength by now.

Still, if people were in places they shouldn't have been...

Including myself in this scenario. Because I shouldn't have opened that door.

"I'm sorry, Damion. But your nephew and your niece

have had a hard week. They lost their mama. Do you want them to lose their grandma too?"

I noticed the hand holding the gun was shaking, like Damion was trying to have some self-control. "Those kids don't need to be with her. She tried to poison them against Theo. Every time Theo comes to get his kids, he has to fix the damage. He had to explain to his little kids that he loved them and he would be there for them. Just because he told Sondra he didn't want to be with her, she didn't have to push her bitterness onto the kids." Damion pointed the gun towards Gladys, "That woman, she encouraged it. I know she did because she's an evil—"

I held up my hands, alarmed by the increasing agitation in Damion's voice and body. "Okay, I'm so sorry. Please calm down. People do incredibly ugly things, especially people who've been hurt."

"Hurt? Sondra caused more hurt to people with her mouth than anybody I knew. She's always been ready to gossip about someone. Lately, she was trying to be a snitch too."

Snitch? What did Damion mean by that?

I didn't have time to contemplate that part anymore because what I'd been waiting for was on the way.

Damion cocked his ear and listened. Then he looked at me. "What did you do?"

"Nothing, I've been talking to you."

"You called the cops some kind of way."

I didn't know what I'd done, but I hoped that we would all be alive when the cops got here.

"I'm not trying to go back to jail." Just like that, Damion took off.

Fear shook me. "Damion. Wait, give yourself up. Don't do anything crazy."

That boy was going to get himself killed.

Chapter 27

I remained shrouded by the web of fear, now more for the troubled young man that had just fled the scene. I heard a commotion at the door. One deputy bypassed me, probably seeing Damion fleeing out the back of the house. Another one saw me.

I waved my hands, "She needs help. I think she hit her head. This woman had a heart attack last week. I know she can't be doing good."

The female deputy walked up to me. "The ambulance is on the way. Ma'am, are you hurt?"

"No, I'm fine." I was still worried about Damion taking off.

I wanted to collapse, so I sat down heavily on the bed and prayed.

I'm not sure how long I waited before two paramedics came through. One walked over to me, but I swatted him away. "I'm fine. She needs your help."

"Eugeena."

I looked to find Amos in the doorway followed by Detective Wilkes.

I'd never been more happy to see two people.

Amos reached down and hugged me. "Are you okay?"

"Yes, I'm fine. Damion took off. I hope they don't hurt him."

Detective Wilkes responded, "Damion is fine and in custody."

"What, you got him that fast?"

Amos answered, "There was backup outside, he wasn't going to get too far."

"Well, did you hear anything?" I suddenly remembered my phone.

Amos grinned, "I heard, but you didn't dial my phone number."

"What?" I pulled my phone out to see who I had dialed. My mouth fell open. "Detective Wilkes?"

She nodded, "Your call came just as we were looking for Damion anyway."

"You knew he killed Sondra?"

"No, at least not until your phone call which we heard from one side. I guess I owe you for helping us solve another murder." Wilkes looked at Amos. "I need to question Damion down at the station. Be sure to get your wife home. We can catch up tomorrow with statements. It's good your lawyer was able to get Briana released today. Of course, the charges will be dropped."

Amos nodded, "Sounds good, Wilkes." He turned to me. "You heard her, let's get you home, woman. I thank the Lord for watching over you. You don't seem to know how to avoid trouble."

I was thankful too. I held onto Amos's arm until we reached his truck. Then I remembered, "What about my car?"

"Don't worry. I called Cedric. He and Carmen will get your car back to the house. You best be prepared for your children to get on you." He sighed, "I guess they will be all over me too since all this started with Briana."

Once we were down the road, "Why were the cops looking for Damion even though they hadn't connected him to Sondra?"

"For J.C.'s murder. It seems those two guys had been at each other's throat since high school. Both have been in and out of prison. Something went down last Saturday at the Black Diamond and Wilkes suspects Damion ended the dispute, fatally."

"Was Damion caught on the Black Diamond's cameras?"

Amos nodded, "Yeah, not for the murder. Damion was seen getting into an altercation with J.C. The owner, Mac Porter, had asked him to leave."

"So Damion left and came back?"

"More like he never left. I believe he sat in the parking lot seething and waited on J.C. to come out."

"But no one heard or saw the shooting outside?"

"No one has come forward."

"He had a gun."

Amos glanced over at me, "You saw a gun? He had it out while you were there?"

"Yeah, I'm thankful to the Lord. For some reason Damion spilled his story to me at least towards the end, then he got agitated again about something." I thought back. "I wonder if Sondra knew what Damion did? She was there the same night. He mentioned something about her being a snitch."

Amos shook his head, "It's possible, but we will never know."

I frowned, "If it wasn't that, I think Sondra had something on Theo and probably Damion. He broke into the house, Amos. He had to be there looking for something. I don't know what Sondra had, maybe it was a photo or a diary. You should let Wilkes know."

"That makes sense. I was wondering why he was there."

"He also explained his bond with Charlene. Damion felt responsible for her sister getting shot. The bullets were meant for him. I wonder if J.C. White had anything to do with what happened a decade ago."

Amos shook his head, "There was a lot of hate traveling around with this group of young people. I hope the remaining classmates find some peace."

I added, "Especially Briana. I'm so glad she can put all this behind her now."

Amos smiled, "Thanks to you. She told me earlier that she really appreciated you stepping up and helping her out. I think things are going to be alright. I know they've been awkward since we got married, but I'm feeling better now. How about you?"

I grinned back, "Much better. Now maybe we can get back on track with a few things."

"I hear you, Mrs. Jones."

I threw my head back and laughed.

It felt so good to laugh.

Thank you, Lord!

Epilogue

Two weeks later, August

It was sort of a family reunion. The Pattersons and the Jones. Alexa had arrived with Douglas two days ago. They stayed over in the house with Briana. My whole family was in attendance. Junior and his family traveled down from Greenville for the weekend. So, my house was full for a change.

Amos started early with cleaning fish for one of his famous fish frys. After stuffing ourselves with food, I gave instructions to a trusted teen at our church. She would be in charge of watching the kids while we traveled down to the Sugar Creek Cafe.

Now we all sat, Alexa, Junior and Judy, Cedric and Carmen, Leesa and Chris.

Even Jocelyn was there with a man. I didn't even know she was dating. I would have to get with Louise about this new development later.

Briana told me earlier that she has not seen Theo in weeks. Probably for the best since he'd been working with his brother's defense lawyer. Damion would more than likely serve a life sentence. Two people died that night.

One, Damion had beef with for a long time and one who'd given his brother grief.

Gladys was spending time in a rehabilitation center. She not only had the heart issues, but the fall had resulted in some brain injury as well.

Theo had official custody of his children. I wasn't sure how that would go, knowing their uncle was responsible for their mother's death.

I felt most sorry for Charlene. The Brown sisters have kept me in the know about their cousin. In many ways Charlene was an accomplice to Damion's crime that night. She knew what happened between Damion and Sondra, but still made an effort to frame Briana. There was a side to Charlene that longed to avenge her sister's death. The sad thing was the guy she was protecting was the root cause. Apparently she'd been taken to a facility after having a mental breakdown.

Amos touched my hand, "Are you okay?"

I smiled. My knight in shining armor checking on me. "I'm good. Just thinking about the events from last month still. A lot of heartache."

"I know." He patted my hand, and then stretched his arm around the back of my chair. "Let's enjoy the night."

The cafe owner, Fay, came out dressed in a stunning copper gold sundress. "We want to welcome one of our very own here at Sugar Creek Cafe to the stage. Here to provide some songs for the evening is the very talented Briana Jones."

Briana was in her element, dressed in black jeans and a olive green short sleeve shirt. We had been talking more. Some of the tension that plagued us seemed to have dissolved. Briana even confided in me where she had gone those few days, something that she hadn't even revealed to

Amos or the police when questioned. She went off to St. Helena Island, which was off the coast of Beaufort, about eighty miles from Charleston.

Her mama grew up on the island when she was younger. The folks there spoke Gullah or Geechee. A few folks in Charleston also fancied speaking the language which mixed West African and English. The house and land where Francine had been raised had been passed down to her daughters. Neither daughter ventured to the humble house on the island, not until a few weeks ago when Briana was looking to get away.

She told me, "I hadn't thought of that house in years. When I left to go find it, I wasn't sure if I could. Once I was there, it was like I felt my mama and her ancestors. I prayed, and I haven't done that in a long time."

I blinked back tears as I recalled Briana sharing her experience with me. Afterwards we prayed together, a bond established between us.

I watched as Briana beamed at the audience, her face appeared fresh and beautiful under the stage's light. "I want to thank Fay for having me here tonight. Thank you for letting me be a part of the Sugar Creek Cafe family. She's been asking me to sing for some time now. To be honest, I lost my desire to sing for a while. And a few weeks ago I didn't know if I would have an opportunity like this again."

She held her head down. When she lifted it, her eyes shone with tears. "My mama used to say 'Ain't God good.'"

The audience responded, "All the time."

Briana perched her guitar on her knee. "I believe that with all my heart even more so. My family is here tonight."

We all hooted and shouted like we were at a ball game.

"My dad remarried earlier this year and my family's been extended. I'm grateful for all of them." Briana sucked in a breath. "I miss my mama, but I know she's looking down on me and I feel like she would approve of the new person in my life. I'm dedicating this first song to Eugeena. You being in my corner has meant the world to me and I know I haven't always embraced you but I want you to know I appreciate you."

I think someone was cutting onions near me because my eyes flooded with tears. I tried wiping them away with my hands.

Amos pressed his handkerchief into my hands.

Now that's a gentleman right there. My husband!

As Briana sang, "Thank you, Lord, for all you've done for me." I glanced over at my husband. Amos's eyes were shining bright as he beamed with pride for his youngest daughter. They both had entered a new direction the past few weeks.

As for me and Amos, married life had never been better.

About the Author

Tyora Moody writes soul-searching mysteries with a dash of romance. Her books include the Eugeena Patterson Mysteries, Serena Manchester Series, and the Victory Gospel Family Series. When Tyora isn't working for a literary client, she enjoys reading, spending time with family, binge-watching crime shows, catching a movie on the big screen, and traveling. To contact Tyora about reviewing her books or book club discussions, visit her online at TyoraMoody.com.

Books By Tyora Moody

EUGEENA PATTERSON MYSTERIES
A Simmering Dilemma, Book 4 (this book)
A Blended Family Christmas: A Short Story
Lemon Filled Disaster, Book 3
Oven Baked Secrets, Book 2
Deep Fried Trouble, Book 1
Shattered Dreams: A Short Story

REED FAMILY SERIES
Relentless Heart, Book 3
Troubled Heart, Book 2
Broken Heart, Book 1

SERENA MANCHESTER SERIES
Bittersweet Motives, Book 2
Hostile Eyewitness, Book 1

VICTORY GOSPEL SERIES
When Perfection Fails, Book 3
When Memories Fade, Book 2
When Rain Falls, Book 1